To

Lu

Thank you

ARaway

15-8-2022

And So It Begins

And So It Begins

For evil men and women to succeed it takes good men and women to do nothing.

ANN R QUAY

For more information, contact: annrquayauthor@gmail.com

FIRST EDITION

ISBNs
978-1-80227-621-3 (eBook)
978-1-80227-622-0 (paperback)
978-1-80227-623-7 (hardback)

Contents

Prologue

*"For evil men and women to succeed it takes
good men and women to do nothing".*

A world torn by division, smothered by corruption and greed, emotions and anger driven by social media and divisions fed upon by the many media empires.

A world governed by a political infrastructure that makes living in The Matrix more a reality than the fiction that movie was meant to be. Born with an ID number and indoctrinated into a, so called, civil society with very little choice of true freedom.

In such a world time would take a toll on many of those who had lived a long enough life to have encountered sadness, frustration, anger and possibly deep sorrow of loss on occasions in their journey through the modern matrix.

Decent hard working people would continue to show their anger and frustrations, a fuse lit by "the straw that broke the camels back".

This fuse had been lit first in many of the younger generation. That fuse igniting in uncontrolled and unreasoned bloodshed. After all, at such a young age, how indeed could a fuse have been created in such a short journey through life's troubled times.

All that was needed was a bigger straw to break the back of just a few mature intellectual individuals. Individuals who may not even have met but whose frustrations of the seemingly ability to do nothing would surface like a tidal wave and commence a domino effect.

A sudden realisation that unless you were of any political importance, a billionaire or a celebrity with the entourage of millions of social media indoctrinated followers, there was little you could do to change the world.

The realisation that your fears of the only option to draw real attention to deal with the issues that caused such deep anger and frustration was to embark on an illegal path. A path that utilised the very media and the corrupt and inadequate political and corporate infrastructure that was the cause of life's anger.

Frustrations shared by many across the world but equally personal significance to many. Each individual capable of previously never thought of acts of disobedience and illegality – even potentially causing death. After all, a good death was certain to attract the worlds many strands of media.

After the world was locked away in their homes, dictated to do so by the political elite and enforced to do so by a police regime united across the world to control the movement of citizens, the straw had become sufficiently large enough giving citizens so much time to reflect and plan.

The first Domino was about to fall, the era of disobedience was coming. Coming in a way never thought possible or achievable but coming it was and the world would be united and divided in a way never encountered on such a scale.

And so it begins . . .

CHAPTER 1

Domino 1

I t was an extremely hot and unusually silent day in the Kruga National Park.

Tanya Wild was her typically enthusiastic self, readying for her next big trophy kill on the hunters private game reserve. She had her mind set on a majestic male Lion, one of the biggest seen crossing the exclusive reserve for those rich enough to afford the minimum $50,000 hunt fee.

For Tanya it wasn't just the excitement of the ultimate kill, it was the glory she adored through her social media postings. Yes there was an equal amount of outrage thrust at "the evil bitch" but her ego was plenty large enough to swallow all the names and hatred under the sun hurled at her.

She was grinning to herself thinking of the onslaught she would receive upon a successful hunt and follow up photo shoot with her lifeless King of the jungle under her thighs. Oh so many possible headline captions to write for that!

Tanya only hunted alone other than with her two regular guides – Ade Abebe and Frank Pearson. Ade was a black African and had been on Kruger National Park for most of his young 38 years. He was short at 5ft 7 but stocky and well built with incredible deep brown eyes. A Christian family man with three children (two girls and one boy) he was at odds with his role as a hunters guide. In fact, if he were to be honest, he would say he loathed the whole enterprise of trophy hunting but the salary was good for a home grown African man needing to look after 3 children. So he swallowed his conscience each and every day but tried hard to ensure he was a kind and helpful as possible to all of the animal treasures he had the fortune of also protecting outside of the hunters licence to kill.

He was no big fan of Tanya. He loathed her social media circus and ensured his children never followed the stories of Tanya Wild. She was probably one of the most famous and infamous hunter customers and as such she tipped well. A successful hunt of the "Majestic One", his own name for the king of the largest pride of Lions in Kruger, would indeed mean a larger bonus than normal. Today though his conscience was having a mighty battle that he knew he would find difficult to keep hidden when the time came. He knew the lies told by politicians and the wealthy that trophy hunting was necessary as part of the financial need to keep endangered species from extinction. He always wondered why the media had never taken up this issue in more investigative detail bearing in mind the huge following anti trophy hunting had across the world.

Frank Pearson was the complete opposite, a tall white South African and a keen trophy hunter himself and indeed one of Tanya Wilds' followers. In fact he fancied and fantasised over Tanya. There was nothing in-depth about Frank's personality, money and a kill and a fit woman was good enough to keep him sleeping well at night.

Tanya liked to think of herself as an Amazon warrior, a true Wonder Woman. She had flowing blonde hair but always tied up under a large camouflage baseball cap for hunts. She was 5ft 9 tall and had an athletic physique supported by media worthy boobs and the perfect selfie, no filter required, face. She was an arrogant American socialite and was far more comfortable in company of "birds of a feather". However, when it came to the hunt anyone and anything was fair game, especially if it boosted her social media watch and comment count.

"Hey boys, are you ready to mount up" she called out with a temptress tone to taunt Frank, whom she knew would love to make her his trophy.

"Yes Miss Wild, ready to walk out when you are, the wind is going to be high at times, have you remembered to be odour neutral?" Ade responded, knowing that the hunter temptress, as experienced as she was, could never not help attract in the male species of her own kind for another type of kill.

Frank responded, to no surprise to Tanya or Ade, with "I'm ready for the ride when you are".

If the track and hunt went as planned it could mean at least 3 days in the various jungle lands of the hunting reserve. Travelling was therefore not light with camping, food and cooking equipment as well as the rifles and ammunition.

"Ade, when did you last see or hear of his majesty's position and do you think we will track him in 3 days" Tanya asked enthusiastically but with an overtone of a demand rather than a question.

Ade responded In his deep but soothing African tone "I saw him ten days ago just outside the reserve Miss Wild but he usually leads his pride onto the reserve when the Gazelle are in numbers near a common watering hole. If he keeps to a similar routine then yes I think 3 days will be ideal".

"That's perfect then because I've got a plane to catch end of next week and a social media shoot based on the success of this expensive outing with you" came the response in the usual self-centred manner.

Tanya was not aware that she was the not the only hunter following her prize victim on this hunt and likely that if she was, it would just have boosted her ego that little more. A typical stance from a person only viewing every aspect from the perspective of her view point. A misunderstanding that could cost her dearly.

The trek through the various terrains over the following days were of no surprise to this trio of jungle experts. They each had noticed animals of all dangers, on their journey, lurking and hiding which the inexperienced explorer would never be aware. A lack of awareness that could indeed have made them the prey.

Ade was pretty sure it was only he though who had noticed the beautiful black female panther in the darkness of undergrowth. It was stealthily moving amongst the jungle undergrowth without making any sound, it was like velvet paws walking on velvet carpet. It was only the fleeting glimpse of the eyes that alerted Ade to this spectacular creature and noticed the female was a new mother and she was cleverly carrying 3 young babes in her mouth slinking down into a dark hole beneath a huge fallen tree. It was blackness walking into the security of blackness.

Ade was secretly pleased that he was sure he was the only one who noticed and was thrilled that the Panther had not become the new or additional ideal trophy for the Amazon queen.

It was on the third day when Frank became aware of the presence of the majestic one. Although Ade was by far the most experienced tracker, Frank being more of an additional security guard in his company, it was Frank who signalled the target first.

He did not speak but just put his left hand flat and slowly in the air to signal a stop, like a military exercise. His right index finger was across his lips to signal silence and then he pointed ahead and to the right.

They were in a fairly heavy tree area all around but about 100 metres to the right was a small watering hole with a couple of large fallen trees at one edge.

The King was indeed majestic, one of the biggest male lions on the reserve if not the biggest. His huge golden frame was stretched longways on one of the fallen trees as he soaked in the morning sunrise, his mane, so long, seemed to be undulating like waves of the sea even though there was very little wind that day.

The excitement and amazement of the size of her prey was clear to see in the bright coldness of Tanya Wilds eyes.

Franks excitement was equal and he was pleased it was he who first spotted the end prize.

As usual Ade could only ever feel the huge drain of mixed emotion and sadness whilst needing never to portray that feeling to his employer.

There was no need of any talk necessary by any of these three. The routine and silent behaviour was embedded in them.

Silently, Tanya had removed her treasured hunters rifle, a rifle she knew would be worth a fortune to those other hunters following her social media. To own the rifle of Tanya Wild, what a trophy indeed. She positioned herself in a standing position resting her rifle on a perfectly situated rock and looked at her prize through the monogrammed "TW – Hunter" specially made telescopic lens.

There was chatter amongst the birds and various species of monkey over head but this did not seem to be signalling any danger to the intended victim.

Ade and Frank had crouched down to their own view point so it was only the head of Tanya Wild that could be seen by those with a keen eye.

Tanya held her breath as she released the safety, closed one eye and gently pushed the rifle into her shoulder ready to take the shot. The jungle seemed to go on silent pause in a dramatic sadness and prayer of the event to take place, a silence that Tanya thought was more of an alert of danger than the previous jungle chattering.

An experienced hunter could tell when Tanya was ready to pull the trigger and as she went to do so the bullet she would never see sent her flying to the floor as it exited her visible head.

The jungle went into uproar, his majesty and his pride sped off shouting their warnings to any creature around that they were on the move and fast.

Ade and Frank fell down on their knees in both misbelief and utter shock.

Frank said to Ade "Did you see anything, where did that come from, what the fuck do we do now?"

Ade responded "I did not see a thing, my whole concentration was on the lion, is she is really dead? We can't move out too far as the pride will be on attack mode and every creature knows we are here. I will radio into base and tell them and see what the next steps are. They will want us to stay here and wait for the local police.

Yes, despite their experience of death of large creatures, this was the first time they had experienced the death of their own kind by the same means they inflicted. It was indeed a sickening shock and sight.

In the distance, about 1,000m, another huntress by the name of Sonia Parker had speedily and silently exited her position in a tree. A tree so perfectly shaped and placed to see the full stretch of trees that the other hunters were in.

She knew she had to exit as quickly and as invisibly as possible. She took with her the satisfaction of the demise of "the evil bitch", the planning of her next moves and the sadness and shock that this is what she had become, what she had been driven to.

She took with her also the thought that she of all people was possibly Domino No 1. If she was then she knew it had begun, and if she carried out the next stages of her plan it was she who definitely would know.

In her head she repeated a phrase stated by an unusual traveler she had met a few years ago, a traveller who had mentioned the possibility and likelihood of the domino effect.

The phrase was:-

> *"for evil men and women to succeed it takes*
> *good men and women to do nothing".*

CHAPTER 2

Sonia Parker
(Domino 1)

Sonia Parker was in her late fifties. An extremely fit, attractive, born and bred Christian African woman. Many would a-liken her to the character Columbiana in the movie about a child who grows to be an assassin.

It was so strange in her mind right now that she actually thought of her friends comments about this comparison but in no way would they ever actually see her as an assassin. Now here she was an actual real life Columbiana assassin.

She had lived a good life and despite her hatred of hunting and her immense passion for all animal kind, the journey of her youth had led her to become a superb marksman.

This experience was born in her early teens when her father would teach her how to shoot small bird fowl for their meals. Such feathered fowl were in abundance in Africa in view of the dwindling predator population of all feline species. The eradication of habitat and the explosion of poaching and legalised trophy hunting had led to their demise. Extinction of any animal kind was never considered genocide by humans but she had never thought otherwise.

At 18 she joined the African military and her already learnt rifle skills quickly made her the perfect candidate for sniper and jungle training. Once she left the military she became part of the African ladies warrior warden patrols to help stem the tide of poaching. Although she had on many occasions confronted poachers and used her weapon defensively she had never, to this day, killed another human being.

At the age of 40 she left her careers to spend as much time with her daughter Naomi and long time husband Sam.

Naomi was a treasure of a human being and at an early age had adopted her mum and dads passion for all animals and the belief they had the right to exist as much as any human being.

It was this passion that led Naomi to become involved in many volunteer protest roles across the world during her time as a relentless youth traveller.

One such protest took her to the blood red waters of Taiji Japan. This is where the Japanese captured and slaughtered, by hand, up to 20,000 dolphins every year. The cove that was the final prison for these beautiful swimming mammals would literally turn blood red.

Naomi ventured there with other volunteers from around the world to help support the famous Sea Shepherd crew who relentlessly risked their own lives on board this ship to protest actively all those at sea who slaughtered their, born to swim, friends.

This trip was one too far for those who cared and had a sensitive nature. For Naomi it was way too far for her young heart and head to comprehend. From her view point above the cove waters she stood and watched helplessly as the screams of the battered, but still alive, dolphins echoed through the early evening air. She imagined their calls to be not only of pain but of distress and also a warning for others to swim for their lives, mum and dad dolphins hoping their children had escaped.

She, like many, broke down in her own hellishly loud screams of pure helplessness, the sickening sight of utmost cruelty and blood soaked abusers willingly hammering blow after blow.

Helpless, breathless from crying and tears that would not stop, screaming without knowing what to scream. In desperation she video called her mum and dad.

They both answered the call and immediately tears welled in their eyes as they could see those in the eyes of their daughter. Once Naomi had finally managed to intake air her first screaming words were "DAD, MUM LooooK – they are slaughtering them LISTEN to the screams

– PLEEEEAASE MAKE IT STOP, PLEEASE Do Something! PLEASE PLEASE I BEG YOU. Oh mum dad – loook – I can't take it".

Before Sonia or Sam could respond the battery life of Naomi's phone had also ran out and the connection was as bluntly terminated as the lives of the dolphins.

That would be the last words and last time that Sonia and Sam would see and hear from their beautiful daughter and wonderful human being.

That whole event was too much for the hardy protester of adult age let alone a teenage novice protester at such a blood thirsty event.

After her call with her parents abruptly ended the urge for her to do something was so overwhelmingly strong. So, when other protesters decided to run down to the cove and rush the slaughterers she literally had no choice. She was driven by anger, frustration, shock and sheer lack of control of thought other than "Do something, Stop it". As the protesters rushed the quickly assembled human blockade of fisherman across the cove Naomi burst through, she was an incredibly athletic young woman and super fast, she tripped and hit her head on a large stone and immediately fell unconscious in the blood thick choking waters.

Naomi never survived that event, she never knew that her death that night had been the one thing that stopped the annual slaughter that year. The Japanese were quite an indignant nation when it comes to traditions but even their Government could not ignore the media and worldwide outcry and publicity of the death of Naomi.

Unfortunately Naomi's death was not the only tragedy of that night which would launch Sonia into a different journey of her life and help become the assassin of one Tanya Wild.

Sam could not suffer the loss of his only child, his beautiful, beautiful girl. He was a very proud decent man and was always able to help his daughter. That night though her screams of help would never stop, never. Nightmares after nightmares and the sheer unacceptable fact that HE COULD NOT HELP and his child died.

So it was only a few years after that dreadful event that despite his Christian upbringing and his immense love for Sonia he could take the mental anguish no more and took his own life by the hands of his own rifle.

Sonia Parker was now on her own and for her the demons doubled and grew every day. She understood Franks anguish and feeling of helplessness but how on earth could he leave her alone, not just in her pain of their daughter but now alone with the pain of losing him.

And that demon that grew, that demon who loathed the Japanese for their ridiculous need for Dolphin food, the callous unforgiving way of their slaughtering and knowing that children like her beautiful Naomi looked on in anguish.

So like many across the world, left on their own, carrying their demons, she sought sanctuary in travelling. There was comfort as well as sadness to think that it was the sorrow of her daughter that led her to follow her young footsteps and explore the world for comfort and individual sanctuary away from all the madness of the modern matrix world.

It was on one of these journeys that she was to meet the traveller. A person who for the first time would mention the possibility of a domino effect by many who would follow the disobedience of others in an eager thirst to vent to the world all that was so obviously wrong.

Sitting by the riverside on a white water adventure one of her fellow rafters approached in a kindly manner and said "do you mind if I sit and join you and if you like I happen to have a bottle of wine you are welcome to share".

Sonia had smiled her brilliant white smile and sensed the calm friendship of the travellers approach.

He looked younger than her, she thought, but was surprised to find out he was nearly ten years older and in his sixties.

His mannerism and ability to listen, more than talk, was calming. It was not long after joint enthusiasms to the past days adventures of the white water rafting trek that he had said "I sense there is some deep sorrow that brings you on this adventure alone. I don't want to pry but I will assure you that you are not alone in your troubles. It is likely every individual on this trip has, to coin a song, 'packed all their troubles in an old kit bag and smiled'. "Probably false smiles" he added.

She could not explain it but this stranger could extract sorrows like a magnet would attract iron shavings. There was something so honest and calming about his nature that any question would not feel like prying.

So the traveller listened and listened intently as Sonia revealed all her life's journey and the horrors that had begun her journey alone, a journey where she hoped she could forget.

She was quietly taken aback in her thoughts as the traveller had obvious knowledge of Taiji and its Dolphins as well as the protesters and the many followers of the Sea Shepherd.

The traveller had said "Sonia you will never forget and nor should you, but people like these with you now and millions across the world have their sorrows and these journeys they take are not to forget but to realise you are not alone".

He went on to many of the other issues across the world from the endangered animals, to the financial collapse and financial imbalance. Of how there was enough money and food for everyone in the world but just not in the right places.

She had realised that the traveller had touched on so many subjects that not only bothered her but many of her own friends. She was fascinated how he explained that the world wide media was a big part of the disease but that one day they would be the cure. Not only fascinated but surprised and intrigued how one person could cover so simply many of the worlds issues and make them solvable and in such a short space of time that you would not have realised.

Time did pass though and not only did that bottle of wine empty but when the traveller offered another Sonia was quick to say "yes please" as for the first time in a long time she did not feel alone.

After the traveller had suggested they better retire or the other rafters will start gossiping "as people always will do" he said, which made her laugh, Sonia agreed.

She left with the various topics of conversation whizzing in her head. She particular reflected on how he had said "millions across the world have similar conversations every day, over breakfast lunch and dinner. Many driven by the news or media stories the night before or that morning. News and stories reminding them of how helpless they are in their tiny part of the exclusive world they exist in. One day an event will take place, an event of disobedience to shock the world, this will cause a domino effect and where we travellers find comfort together others will find comfort that they are not the only domino. It will be an era of disobedience from the mature educated population who have suffered enough too many times". He had ended with:-

"for evil men and women to succeed it takes good men and women to do nothing".

Sonia slept better that night but her thoughts would stay with her for a long time, in fact forever, in fact they were the thoughts right with her as she took that shot and set the first domino into that evil bitch.

Although Sonia felt some disbelief that she had actually undertaken an act of murder her guilt was diminished by the thoughts that whizzed through her mind. She knew though that her plan was not over and that eventually the media and the public would decide the level of her guilt. It did not really matter to her though as she set out on this path knowing that for her, this was justified. She did not do nothing, she was not helpless, it was not Japan but it was her territory and therefore it was up to her to do something.

She had secretly followed the majestic lion for months, she knew Kruga like the back of her hand. Once she found a spot she took a well educated guess that is where the lion would sit and where Tanya Wild would make her kill. She scouted all the surrounding area looking for the best possible shots from one position. It was not hard for her to get to know the itinerary and booking days of the hunter guides and it was made more obvious by the social media bragging of Tanya about who and when her next kill would be "watch this space folks!" she had bragged. Sonia was watching that space all right!

Needing to try and be undiscovered she wanted to leave as few tracks as possible so she had found a way to travel near 400 metres through the trees, like Tarzan and Jane, to end in a tree some 1,000m from her ideal shooting range. She had patiently waited 2 days in that spot, nothing for a warrior warden with the experience of waiting in expectation of catching poachers over a much much longer period.

She knew the guides would not make any sudden moves because of the worry over the fleeing lions and other unseen predators. This bought her the time to smoothly dismantle her rifle into a small ruck suck and slink across to another tree. Her movements would never be noticed 1,000m away by the naked eye and more likely to be seen as a monkey or bird.

When she had made her way to the her exit tree she changed her small size 5 sneakers into some hand filled size 9 men's boots. From this point on the tracks she would leave, for maybe another 4 miles, via her own untrodden paths, would be by a size 9 man according to her foot prints.

Once home she found herself to be calmer than she expected although feelings of guilt had increased slightly but that would not deter her. She was mature enough and angry enough to know that if she was likely to feel immense guilt and not be able to justify with herself that she would never have proceeded. What finally pushed her to be Domino 1, the final straw, is when Tanya Wild added a video to her social media. The caption was "it's only Dolphins people!". The place was Blood Cove, Japan.

Now for her next stage of a plan. A letter to the Editors of three major news papers in America, Canada, U.K., Australia, Germany and Africa. The letter was the same.

"Dear Editor,

Today I conducted the hunt of the infamous trophy hunter, Tanya Wild. It is not for me to explain my reasons just yet.

However, there is a great story here and one which I will tell.

First though, you are in the position of preventing the demise of another trophy hunter.

*All you need to do is allocate one journalist, a good honest investigative journalist to write a feature article on **Trophy Hunting and other animal slaughters,** this is to include names of the famous hunters, celebrities, politicians, royalty etc. Their rationale.*

It is to include proper investigative details of the finances involved and where the finances go.

There is added value to you if you include comments from celebrity anti hunters and their solutions to the killing and of course extra points if you get any politician to record their views of the benefits or not of the 'sport.'

The rest is up to your journalist and the prize for the winning article is . . . a one to one interview with me and exclusive photos of my journey to hunt one Tanya Wild.

Your article must be a featured article and it must be published in your tabloid and on line version with options for readers comments and likes open.

This feature article must be released 60 days from now in the week commencing 1st May 2023.

You must also print a copy of this entire letter of my demands in your next available publications.

Winners will be notified by post – the judges decision is final.

To my fellow travellers out there – this is Domino 1 signing off.

Ps "for evil men and women to succeed it takes good men and women to do nothing"

Sonia had used an old mobile phone with an old font to write the letter and print them in mass on a small portable printer. The envelopes were addressed with stickers produced via the same printer.

She had posted them at the same time but from a post box several hours away from her home town. Distance enough to cover anyone wanting to try and track back to an area by the receiving post office stamp.

She had no intention of making another kill and she was confident that just the suggestion of such would be the added story incentive the media needed. Confident enough that the reaction to her first letter would create world wide chattering of the human kind.

Now she would sit back and watch and watch. She had well and truly done something, that was for sure.

What she was not sure about though was whether any of the millions of readers out there would understand her signing off as Domino 1. It would not be long before she knew at least one person did, in addition to the traveller of course, and she wondered if indeed if the traveller' was still alive.

CHAPTER 3

Whodunnit

Ade and Frank were now flat on their stomachs. Frank said to Ade in a loud clenched whisper "We need to stay low as the shooter might be looking at us, also we have to cover Tanya's body soon as the smell of her blood will soon attract feeders".

Ade acknowledged so they both lay flat looking out into the distance where they thought a shot may have come from.

Tanya lay lifeless just feet away to which both guides eyes constantly strayed back and forth to. After about ten minutes of eagle eye gazing they were sure the shooter had left and it was Ade who stood up first to take greater stock of any other creatures that might have returned or stayed in hiding. He signalled to Frank to stand whilst simultaneously clicking the call button on his sophisticated guides radio. It usually had good reception over a very long distance.

It was only a few seconds before central guide control answered "hello Ade how is the hunt going? Is everything ok?" came the response from Sharma, a long time friend of Ade and an expert guide as well as a passionate animal protector. She actually was a warrior warden with a friend called Sonia Parker who had now left the employed service.

Ades voice was not that of his usual calm self as he responded "Sharma, no something terrible has just happened Miss Tanya has been shot and is dead".

"What! Accidentally shot? – by whom and how? – are you kidding!?" Came the disbelief response.

"Sharma no, she was hunted herself, Frank and I could not see anyone but I would say she was shot from a long way out. We need to move her body out quickly because of the smell of blood, can you send a jeep to nearer our position and call the police?"

"Yes of course, oh my goodness, send me your grid reference and I'll be back to you as soon as I can, stay safe."

Frank had heard the conversation and said to Ade "we will have to carry Tanya a couple of miles possibly to another grid reference as the jeep won't be able to get that close to this point".

Ade agreed and mentioned about the police forensics. "There is not a lot they will find, we can outline her body position with stones and other than bringing them to this exact location there is not more to be found" Frank intelligently responded.

So Ade radioed back to Sharma and told her a grid reference they were walking to and why. Sharma responded "yes understood and I was going to suggest that, I've contacted the police, they were astounded, and they will be following me to your pick up point."

"Ok Sharma, see you in a few hours, keep me posted of your progress, over and out".

Although Frank and Ade had to carry the body of Tanya on a quickly made wooden stretcher they made the pick up grid reference, a few miles away, quite a bit before Sharma and the police investigators.

Two officers had arrived in their separate police jeep along with Sharma in the game reserved main emergency jeep.

Ade knew the two officers as they too were locally born and he introduced Frank to them.

The lead officer was Junior Semboa and his first word to Ade, having looked at the lifeless Tanya, was "unbelievable."

He asked Ade if he would lead them to where the incident happened even though he had been out on trek for more than 3 days now. They suggested Frank go back with Sharma with the body of Tanya. They had arranged for other officers to meet them back at central base and take a statement and recover the body to the local morgue for an autopsy.

Both Ade and Frank agreed to the requests and Frank added "I've already taken some pictures of the scene and happy to show them to your officers". The officers said "that is fine" and Ade stood there thinking 'pictures I'm sure you want to sell and also improve your social media hit rate'.

On the journey to the kill site the younger officer, Ben Larson, had asked Ade if he had any ideas of who or how could conduct such a shooting. Ade said "Miss Tanya had many many followers most of which were more enemies than supporters. So the question of 'who' could be a choice of hundreds of thousands. However the question of how would limit that possibility. To undertake such a shot and in that terrain and to vanish, so far, unnoticed would take an expert rifle person and someone who knows Kruger well. Perhaps even an envious fellow trophy hunter whom Tanya had upset by some of her arrogant posts".

The two officers fully understood.

Once they had all returned to the central base a few hours later Ade completed his statement for his officer friends. It was now late evening and getting dark and Ade needed to rest from physical and mental exhaustion and sheer shock.

Before they all retired that night though the officers had explained the next steps. That they would contact Miss Wilds relatives and then report it to the local press as in view of the unknown rationale of this murder there could be other events and therefore control of the publicity was important. Also, they explained they would make another journey to the kill site after speaking to the coroner to try and find any other clues of the shooter.

Finally, but not least, they said that for now all planned Trophy Hunts must be stopped until further investigations are completed. Their advice was to call an emergency meeting of all game wardens in the morning and radio those out on scout missions to be on full alert of any unknown person they may have or will encounter.

Sonia Parker would have felt some comfort that her action, her commitment to do something, had stopped, even just for a short time, Trophy Hunting in Kruger. Naomi would have been proud of her.

None of those involved today could ever have guessed the media storm and attention that was about to unfold.

CHAPTER 4

The Killer Queen is Dead

Sonia Parker's letters to editors had not arrived or been opened before the super fast grapevine of social media had erupted. They say there is nothing to travel faster than light but social gossip was super fast to get across from one side of the world to every other side before darkness had broken in some parts.

It's hard to say how the first post started as there was no official release at this time. Ade suspected that there was a good chance it was Frank as he was a Trophy Hunter and was in most of the same social media groups as Tanya. Frank would want as much of the spotlight he could get. Along the lines of 'I was there so follow me folks'.

Junior Semboa was thankful he had managed to contact Tanya Wilds parents before this electrifying media explosion. Tanya did not have any children and Sonia Parker was aware of that as although she could, in her immense anger and frustration, topple the media legal animal killer, she would not have been able to leave any child motherless.

She sort of thought that Tanya having no children was part of the end fate.

A surprising calm response that came from Tanya's parents had also eased Junior's dreaded task of being the 'death informant'.

Her parents had immediately cried of course and were very distraught but they were not totally shocked. They had warned their daughter of her arrogant nature and had seen the vicious comments and threats to her on a daily basis.

They could not understand how their daughter could not just encourage such anger but relish in it and sometimes taunt both her libellous and slanderous commentators.

Neither parent were hunters or supporters of hunting. It was the rich socialite company and lifestyle Tanya became addicted to that made her the person she was. So many rich hobby hunters taking centre of attention over champagne and olives.

One of the very first posts and probably the most prominent was one on a Trophy Hunters group page. The group page was called 'Will Kill' meant to be some kind of clever play on the movie 'Kill Bill'.

The headline was "The Killer Queen is dead" and there were past pictures of Tanya both dressed in her socialite Queen of the ball, boob prominent gowns, and of her in her camouflages posing with a number of her trophies.

The comments on this post were mainly of shock and lots of discussions between hunters of how and who. Some were more disappointed that they had heard that Kruger had suspended hunts.

Many many other stories followed in quick succession. Talk about gossip and Chinese whispers, the human jungle and it's grapevine was in full full flow right now.

The emotions of the social groups and individuals varied from sadness to shock to exuberant joy.

If you were to measure the worldwide response on day 1 of domino 1 the feeling would have been on the end of the scale where the end read 'good riddance about time'.

One of the most viewed comments was from one of the more famous celebrity anti-trophy hunters – comedian Ricky Gervais. He had simply put "I said the lions needed and would, one day, have a rifle to defend them".

He said no more, no comic picture or meme or witty jokes, which was his temptation, but just those words. He never even mentioned the name of Tanya Wild. His manager had alerted him to the explosion across the media so he knew his audience would either know already of what he was referring to or find out by asking in his comments box on that thread.

His comment box was steadily overflowing and they all knew to what and whom he was referring.

On that same day the daily tabloid "Africa Today" ran a front page section based on news from the local police.

Their headline was "Trophy Hunter – Hunted and Killed in Kruga" pictures were shown of Tanya and small comments taken from Junior, Ade and Frank.

The editorial team had met to discuss this breaking news and it's ramifications in their country. A trophy hunter actually killed, they already had had previous discussions about headlines and copy if a Trophy Hunter had been killed by animals but never shot by another person on purpose.

At this time a letter to the Editor from a certain Sonia Parker had not been received. When it did arrive that editorial team would have another urgent meeting.

Equally across the world in America, Canada, U.K, Australia, Germany and every country the editorial teams had met to discuss the social media chatter and the breaking story.

TV News and radio stations were clambering for the facts and any suitable pictures and backgrounds on anyone connected.

The worlds media machine went into full throttle.

None of them had yet received that letter, none of them knew that they were already pushing domino 1 firmly over.

None of these lifelong media experts would comprehend the media rush and near professional hysteria that the 'pony express' letter would create. The worlds media would have so many angles to contemplate and each rushing for the ultimate unique story.

Every celebrity and politicians comments could be another story in itself.

What the Editors and journalists could never imagine in their many strategically discussed story lines was that domino 2 was soon to fall.

In the safety and comfort of her own sanctuary Sonia Parker read and read and read. It was sooooooo tempting for her to comment on sooooo many posts but she was mature and grounded enough to refrain and control he urges.

She thought of Naomi and of Sam and wanted to say to them 'I finally did something, I'm so sorry I was too late, love you both.'

She had a plan and had to keep to it. She also remembered a traveller she met saying 'one day a trophy hunter will be shot and the world media will have little choice but to make it, for a time, the most talked about subject in the world.'

How right that traveller was she thought.

Tea Break for you readers

Hello readers, it's your new author here.

I want you to take a quick break and have a cup of tea or glass of wine and take time to think in your own way of the media chaos that would take months and many pages for me to put in words.

Whilst you have your drink I want you to become involved in this break out story and imagine the discussions taking place in every single media office, with celebrities, politicians with TV and Radio stations and most of all across every breakfast, lunch and dinner table.

Think ahead of the same issues when those letters arrive and think the same again after every domino falls.

Your own thoughts are going to be as just as real, in fact more real, and just as accurate as my words.

Each and everyone of you will share both similar and different views and that makes you part of this story and gives it some reality for a short while.

When you have had your drink then rejoin me and

I'll finish the story with what I feel are the most pertinent events as the world eventually sees change, the matrix overlords stir and the most spoken phrase for sometime becomes:-

"For evil men and women to succeed it takes good men and women to do nothing"

I hope you enjoy this book as much as your cup of tea or glass of wine.

Now, where were we . . . oh yes media chaos.

Who is Domino 1?

The first paper to receive the letter from Sonia Parker was Africa Today but two other papers in Africa received them shortly after.

It was only the day after these that they all landed at their respective destinations. However, each offices sorting and prioritising of letters to editors varied considerably and also by the diligence of the first person to read the content. This changed the actual timescales of chaos in each receiving office. After all how many letters are received addressed "to the editor" and how often is the Editor the first person to open such a letter?

(Author to readers – remember that drink break 😊)

The reaction that Sonia Parker would have liked the most, if she was a fly on the wall, would have been from the Editor of the Daily Digest – U.K. and of course any other editor doing the same, even though all would eventually take a similar path, but not all.

Yes, Brad Stevens, Editor of the Daily Digest was in early that morning and so was a junior assistant who opened post addressed to the Editor and happened to be an anti hunt side of person.

A young assistant who had aspirations of being a journalist and uncovering world breaking issues by good old blood, sweat and investigative journalism. Yes, young Julie Harper opened this bit of post and was. as they say, "gobsmacked"!

She must have read the letter several times and spilled her coffee whilst doing so. She looked at the envelope for a post mark and stamp, she looked on the reverse, she wondered if the police would want to take finger prints (not that would do any good as Sonia Parker wore gloves to hold and post). Anyhow it was good thinking on her part.

Not only was she gobsmacked but her brain was whizzing as only last night she was with her friends having a glass of wine (or three or six) and they were all discussing the social media chat of the Killer Queen.

If the worlds audience had known who had killed Tanya Wild then most would not know to whom Killer Queen referred to!

The other simple thing that Julie noticed, as most relevant to her career at this point in time, was that at the end the writer had put all the Editors of the other papers he or she had sent this to. This meant, in media headlines terms and first base to stories, that a rush to the post was on.

Rush she did as she noticed that on that day that Brad had arrived early so off she sped, faster than a cheetah, up to the top floor of the editors office in Derry Street, London W8.

Brad was sitting at his desk drinking his usual take away cappuccino surrounded by various copies of newspapers. Standing outside his open door Julie was nearly dance shuffling on the floor with her feet and her right hand was doing the same on the glass of his open door. "Brad, excuse me but I really really do think you need to see this".

For an Editor Brad had quite a calm nature to himself, maybe because he worked so many hours that bought him the times to be calm and he was intrigued by this eager fluttering of "can't wait" by a young employee whom he knew very little of.

He ushered Julie in with a friendly tone and said "you better come in then before you break an arm".

Julie entered and simply thrust the letter into Brad's outstretched hand whilst her face said without any words "see what I mean". Her eyes remained wide open awaiting the immediate facial response from chief man himself.

Although Brad was normally calm this time his face betrayed him. "Oh my god, this literally just came in? was it hand delivered? do you have the envelope"? He questioned.

"Yes just came in, here is the envelope and might I point out all the cc editors Brad".

Now Brad was an out and out newspaperman all his career (aka life) and he had seen hoaxes and copycats and all sorts but this, this he knew was real. He too had, of course, been involved in yesterday's meeting over the social outburst of this event and was secretly wishing he had not been so hasty. The post mark on the envelope showed it was sent before the media outbreak, all the cc's meant he had to really think fast.

"Julie, you and I are in early and my secretary will arrive soon but I need you to help me call all the editorial team now and if they are not on their way in, get them in".

"Yes of course, anything to help".

Brad placed his iPad on the desk and showed the six numbers of the minimum 12 people Brad wanted in his room a.s.a.p. to Julie and she understood and started calling.

For those that Brad called it was easy, they knew it was Brad and they knew they had to be in. Equally they knew it was Brad and therefore this was something big. For Julie the calls were a little bit longer "hi I'm Julie from the office, you might not know me but I'm sitting with Brad Stevens and he has asked me to call you and say he needs you in now for a breaking story" Some actually asked to speak to Brad first, as if it might be a hoax, but Julie Just lifted the phone and whispered to Brad "please shout to come in" Brad shouted "come in! it's urgent".

And so come in everybody did. Twelve eager men and women fully assembled and ready to judge.

Brad was nice enough, before Julie herself asked, to say to her "Julie, thank you, you can stay and listen if you wish as we may decide on a route to keep details of this letter to the minimum of staff".

He could tell how excited she was and quietly smiled as he noticed her feet were still dance tapping.

All finally seated he handed out copies of the letter just received, copies taken by Julie as Brad's secretary had just arrived and was sat outside in an equal early time and a little confused as to what had happened and why was everyone in Brad's office. Still she would find out soon and in the interim she thought she might just log on and see how many thousands of likes and comments that a post from Ricky Gervais had grown by. She called it 'investigative journalism'.

Brad watched the various faces of this hugely experienced editorial team read this short but pretty succinct letter. These faces all told the same story, the main one being that it was truthful. He had seen the faces which expressed 'nonsense and rubbish'. He also noted those that smiled or professionally chuckled at the possibilities and he noticed the one person whom he knew had rattled over a thousand possibilities in their mind before the others had got to the cc's at the end.

It was to Bill Cartwright that Brad first addressed. "Bill your thoughts?"

Bill was a long term journalist and a true professional although over the last 15 years or so he had become despondent with the media in general. Always loyal as he knew how important good journalism was and the value it used to have and could have. Now he felt that the news of a celebrity bonking his wife's best friend or something would attract more views than the sinking of the titanic.

Bill was more enthused about this letter than most and more than he would let on right now and quietly beneath the desk his shoes were doing just as eager dance as Julie's were.

Bill responded "so quickly here are a few pointers for our think tank here".

1. We need to rethink our agreed approach on the Killer Queen topic.
2. The letter I think is real, this means we have a real killer and this means we have to inform the police.
3. There are a lot of cc's so we have to decide whether we communicate with them all or just go solo. That is a big decision.
4. If other cc's go solo they won't want to talk anyway and that then is a big risk as first to press wins the day.
5. The author gave 60 days for investigative reporting.

That means they feel sure they won't be caught in 60 days or don't care if they are.

6. What other Trophy Hunter?

7. It's a big social media sensation already and this has just made it 1,000 times bigger.

8. Can we actually make the decision between us, what political and advertising influence can we tread on?

9. Who on earth is Domino 1 and is there another domino?

10. The letter is real and as a journalist the winners prize is too good not to try and win. The P.S is going to put media on the spot if they do nothing.

That is my quick thoughts? Any other starters for ten anybody?"

Brad grinned as he could see, as usual, that the others, all younger than Bill, were impressed that these thoughts took less than a minute to rattle out. He particularly warmed to Bills overtones on point 10.

"Ok everyone, all good points and I agree this letter is real so I will, but not as quickly as Bill made them, try and answer his points and then get votes and comments, ok?"

1. Killer Queen story – if we publish then the request becomes our main story – we need to watch social media traffic. The author wants peoples opinion for sure.

2. I will inform the U.K. police.

3. We publish the letter tomorrow with a headline in front page. I will also let the other newspapers know late this afternoon that as our first step we have, at least, decided to publish the letter.

4. Dealt with in 3.

5. Good point, we need to keep a good relationship with all police and not be worried about keeping a side story open of the 'hunt for the hunter of the hunter'!

6. Another good point – a 'who is next story' with pictures and backgrounds of fellow trophy hunters in Tanya Wilds social media groups?

7. Yes, we need a person monitoring specifically any social media stories coming out, especially those connected to celebrities and politicians. The publication of the authors letter is, I think, going to ruffle feathers and I also think this is the authors hope.

8. Normally I would say let's reflect but no, we publish and then take stock later if there is any fall out. The danger of not publishing and others do, is a bigger risk.

9. Another good point. Again is there any social media chat that gives mention of dominos or similar. Win the prize and I'm sure we will be told.

10. Good point and if we publish our audience will expect the article, if all the papers publish those expectations will be higher. The other question though is do we unite

with other journalists from those papers as all may well be approaching the same possible story contributors.

Surprisingly there was a unanimous nod of approval and it was Bill who first stood up and said "hey my friends, I'm long in the teeth not long to retire but I've always wanted to get my teeth into a meaty story (excuse any pun) and one of an investigative nature. If you don't mind I would like to run with the feature article and happy that anyone else continues with the Killer Queen death itself. We will need a good foot soldier though to do a lot of the background research, contacts and social monitoring etc".

With that, a nervous little voice with a footstep dance and a wavy hand came from the back of the room as Julie said "I would love to be the foot soldier and I'm already well up on all the social media traffic on Killer Queen. What a rhapsody ay!". Some immediately laughed, some did not quite get the connection with the song by Queen 'Killer Queen'.

Brad said, "I appreciate not everyone has had a say but the signals are that all agree and in view of the critical nature I'm running with as said. Bill you are on and you start now, Julie is yours to use and also for Helen to use. Helen as you were already running the Killer Queen story I want you to continue but now use anything that Bill and a Julie find out as this unravels to continue the story stretch.

So unless there is anything else let's get busy people, there's news to spread.

As they all left the room and before Brad called the police, he read the letter one last time and he wondered (*like I've asked you lovely readers to do*) what on earth was going on in all the other newspaper offices right now.

Equally he reflected on Bills astute question 'why Sign off as Domino 1 and is there a Domino 2'?

He only had to press print on the publication of that letter and he would soon find out.

Whodunnit 2

Scotland Yard inspectors arrived in Brad Stevens office an hour after he made the call. They knew there was little they could do as it was a South African offence but in view of the nature of the letter and the request and that Brad said he was publishing they knew they must respond quickly.

On arrival they simply took the original letter and envelope and asked Brad about the actions he was taking regarding the other media. The fact that they had not obviously been asked to attend at the other two U.K. newspapers who were on the cc list gave him some satisfaction of arriving in very early that day as he was likely to be first past the post. Having said that, he knew full well morning headlines could change rapidly nowadays if the editor so needed them to.

The Inspectors said they would be making contact with the South African police and if the letter was real they would not be the only ones to have approached them from around the world.

The last thoughts of the Inspector were correct as when they managed to get through to the young African detective called Junior he explained they were the 5th such contact out of what appears to be a potential 15.

Junior and Ben had taken Ade back to the scene of the shooting the following day. They already had the quick analysis from the Coroner. Cause of death obvious, looking at the angle of the entry and exit wound he said that as she was standing the assassin must have shot from a height and at an angle down, from a north westerly position of where Tanya was standing and if the location is as told on the police report it was also from quite a way out.

The three of them had spread out about 5 yards apart when they revisited the kill site and had reached the trees in the north west position.

There was a mass of trees and these commenced a long way before the distance they guessed the shooter had taken the shot. They knew there had to be a clear view so they assumed the shot came from a tree on the edges of the tree line but it felt like looking for a needle in a hay stack.

Ade was an experienced tracker but he could not find one foot print in any decent circumference in the guess work of area they thought the shooter must have been in. It was due to rain that afternoon so after that there was no chance of any clues on top of the little chance already.

Strangely enough, but fortunate enough for Sonia, is that as all 3 turned round willing to accept nothing found. If Ade had looked up above his head in the v neck of the branches of a tree about 1,000m away from the kill zone he might have noticed a dark green trodden-on leaf. A leaf that held the shoe print of a size 5 ladies sneaker.

So at this point in time there was actually no or little clue as to whodunnit. Their case may well depend on the news media keeping to their 60 day time limit.

CHAPTER 6

The Twins
(Domino 2)

The Daily Digest was the first in the U.K. to print the letter received by Domino 1. Africa Today's Editor and lead team had also decided to publish the letter although for them the story of The Killer Queen would have to take different connotations.

(remember again that tea or wine break readers ☺)

In fact, all but two of the main recipients decided to print the entire letter. Of course many other publications copied it and reproduced it. The two papers that chose not to print in any timely fashion would not long regret it when their readers had read it in other media and noticed the letter had included the cc list of all those it was sent to.

The publication of the letter kept the chatter of the Killer Queen story as major news and interest and debate across all the same mediums as the initial story of the death of Tanya Wild.

All those actively involved in hunting and anti hunting took more of an interest. Celebrities and Politicians involved and anyone in the finance of trophy hunting took a concerned interest and many were arranging their own breakfast, lunch or dinner meetings along the lines of 'have you had any immediate contact from a journalist yet and if not and you do are you going to comment and if so what'?

Outside of these mass of worldwide readers there were 4 particular readers of interest. One was Sonia Parker, Two was a traveller and Three and Four were a set of twins who took particular interest in "This is Domino 1 signing off".

The twins, identical, Bill and Ben. Yes they cursed their parents for actually naming them William and Benjamin without ever thinking that through their life they would be known as 'the flower pot men! and be asked 'where is little weed'?

They were already engrossed in the story and debate of The Killer Queen but when they read the published letter from Domino 1 they both felt a Deja Vu type of chill.

It could even be an urge they felt, an urge to do something.

This urge they now had was mesmerising, relishing in the social media outburst over Trophy Hunting. They were fascinated equally by the fact it seemed that the majority of the entire worlds population knew exactly why Domino 1 had asked the worlds media to investigate the evil ' sport' they had unleashed their shot on.

William and Benjamin were of high middle class backgrounds and both had made a comfortable amount of money as city software developers, mainly for special projects in the financial world.

Both had married at the same age and both had two, now in their 30's, children.

Their homes were in the same town of Dulwich.

Literally they were two twins in a pod and they preferred jokes along those lines rather than the flower pot men and little weed jibes. Strange though, that following their encounter with the traveller such remarks about their unfortunate link to that old children's tv programme never bothered them. They both always quickly retorted 'heard it too many times, move on' as a way to rebuke the verbal comedian as foolish. It tended to work too.

Life for them, you could say, was pretty comfortable and they could afford the large mortgages on their equally large properties.

In addition, they had sufficient savings to invest in shares and not being high risk takers they chose only to buy shares in reputable financial institutions such as the Bradford and Bingley and Northern Rock building societies. After all these were surely safe as overseen by the then, Financial Services Authority (FSA) under strict rules of solvency etc.

All in their world seemed settled until the year of 2008 when, out of nowhere and in a few short days, the world for most people collapsed. Lives collapsed like dominos in synchronisation with that of the worlds entire banking, building society and mortgage market.

Shares in the financial sector stopped trading and one after one various building societies collapsed and were made insolvent. These included Bradford and Bingley, Northern Rock, Alliance and Leicester, the mighty Halifax and many more in England alone. The main market of America was hit just as hard with just as many "safe" investments being liquidated. The Leman Brothers private bank probably being one of the largest and most famous financial institutions to fall.

Oh yes, 2008 was a bad year all right and all the executives on the boards of all these safe institutions and those at the FSA, had a lot to answer for.

And yet, not one of those mother fuckers did, not one. No jail time, no financial penalty, nothing, they all escaped.

Losing their jobs was nothing at all and not all did. They were all wealthy enough.

To make matters worse the U.K. government bailed out most of these building societies. Bailed them out with U.K. tax payers money. Taxes that the twins had paid and they were not insignificant taxes either!

And then . . . a few years later the Government sells these U.K. owned companies off cheaply to overseas Banks or the larger U.K. ones that survived.

So the shares that they had invested – over £400,000 between them – classed then as worthless were not worthless anymore to the new owners. No the accumulation of these tax payer owned banks into the coffers of other bankers just made them all that more richer.

William had written to the Economic Secretary furiously asking how on earth they could, or had the right to, decide which companies survived or not and only protect the actual savings investors and not the savings of those who purchased shares. The response was just as infuriating, a typical political 'protect your backside, nothing wrong here but apologies' load of waffle.

He had also tried to see which lawyers across any part of the world were conducting class action civil suits against the directors and officers of each of these companies. He found none and received no positive response from any legal firm and yet it was a slam dunk that every board executive was liable for gross negligence of the management of funds.

Their guilt was inescapable.

He knew that the large insurers held their breath as all those institutions had to have Directors and Officers cover for events such as this. It was obvious to both twins though that something was afoot as if the Insurers had to pay out then some of those companies could have been liquidated too possibly. No actuary would have forecast that a whole bloody banking sector had employed incompetent idiots all at the same time to run their ships!

If things could not get any worse it was not much more than a year after that the Government, with the aid of the Financial Ombudsman, were enforcing these saved by taxes, useless banks to pay out hundreds of millions to customers who might have been mis sold a personal accident policy. The era of the PPI, never mind those whose lives were destroyed by loss of savings in shares 'we have used their money to buy the banks and now all you citizens can claim hundreds of millions of pounds from them'!

Where was the lunacy going to end? ' Yes we will bail the banks out with £600 billion pounds of the taxes you have paid, no one will be convicted, you will lose your shares but you can still claim a few hundred million because you was mis-sold a small policy whilst they were all mis-selling mortgages and making everyone broke'!

Millions of hard working people buying houses left with mortgages now far higher than the value of their homes. Not the bankers or the politicians though, oh no.

Nor of course the FSA and other boardroom executives who were given a 'get out of jail free and keep your mortgage free home card'.

There wasn't any real media investigation of what went wrong or trial by Press of all those boardroom buffoons.

THE TWINS (DOMINO 2)

And yet what comes out in 2016? A brilliant movie called The Big Short.

This might as well have been the sole courtroom case for all those lawyers that did nothing. The Big Short nailed everything that was wrong and illegal. It revealed the downright epitome of the evil of Corporate Corruption and greed.

It wasn't just the financial collapse where the movie world highlighted the depth of corporate corruption. Netflix revealed the callous corruption of the Sackler family in Dopesick and the Boeing CEO in 'Downfall the case against Boeing'. In both cases such corporate corruption causing many many deaths and suffering. In both cases those responsible escaped with just huge fines paid for out of the business empires. Not paid for by the individual. No no no.

So in nearly all Corporate corruption cases those responsible walked free, their businesses paid for the corruption, there was no punishment to ever put off other CEO's from following in their footsteps. Prison and substantial financial loss to the individuals responsible was the only solution.

Evil, where good men and woman did nothing.

William and Benjamin were good men, they basically did nothing though and in the same way they lived similar lives together they both lost everything at the same time together.

Their shares investment lost all their spare cash, their jobs were lost because all their work was for the now failed institutions and their huge mortgages were now more than their houses.

Both had strained relationships with their wives. They worked far too many hours. The stress and fall out from 2008 ruptured in divorce for both of them in 2010.

This is when, like many other souls lost on their journey in life's Matrix, the Matrix kicked them out they went travelling together.

Their first escape was a 14 day hiking trek across the width of England known as the Coast to Coast walk or Wainwright's Walk. Approx a total of 190 miles.

On this trek they met, in one of the pubs that hikers stopped at each night in the Lake District, a rather interesting traveller.

They seemed easily to have mentioned their dreadful financial loss following the bank and financial collapse of 2008 and subsequent impact on their lives.

Surprisingly they also vented about Bill and Ben jokes, something they never actually did in gentle friendly chat. It was normally always done in an angry retort.

This traveller had touched on many things and had a great insight to the financial workings of the City. The fact that he had also lost over £50,000 in shares in the Bradford and Bingley made the conversation easier, if that were possible.

During that eye opening and refreshing conversation on many of life's woes the traveller had mentioned a discussion he had with a fellow traveller on a white water rafting adventure. It was about Trophy Hunting and that one day he thought a Trophy Hunter would be shot causing immense media publication and that it would start a domino effect.

The more interesting detail was that he explained how the main media and social media could be used to help ease the worlds frustration and anger and that 'domino events' may well be the impetus for that.

At some point he said 'citizens would understand how to use social media and manipulate those who so far use it to manipulate them and their views.'

His retiring words that night, before they all had to get up early for their next days trek across the beautiful and soothing Lake District, were:-

> *'Guys, we are in a world where for evil men*
> *and women to succeed it takes good men and*
> *women to do nothing'*

That urge they now had was now one of action. They did nothing in 2008 but they were not going to do nothing now. They were going to do something shocking. They, for years, had a plan they called "pay back".

All they needed was a Domino to tip their plan into action.

Step centre stage sharp shooter of Tanya Wild, we are joining your performance.

CHAPTER 7

Pay Back

Yes, 2008 was a long time ago but the twins memory was longer and they had lots of time to plan.

If there was a Richter scale for anger and frustration for others having control of your life then the twins would register over ten.

They wanted to have control over those same or similar people, they wanted to be in control of a collapse. They wanted to make sure corporate corruption, of which gross negligence on scale seen in 2008 was such, was classed as a criminal act punishable by law with a minimum ten year prison sentence.

Now, unlucky for the twins that they worked so hard as highly paid special projects IT developers for the financial world.

Also lucky for the twins that they worked so hard as highly paid special projects IT developers for the financial world.

The latter was definitely not so lucky for the mother fuckers who thought 2008 was long gone and forgotten.

You see the IT world is a bit like cops and robbers. You have hackers (robbers) and fire wallers (police).

There is nothing worse for IT security as a fire waller becoming a hacker. This is especially so when they are as geeky and as good as the flower pot men.

For a few years the boys had been developing and trialling viruses and antidotes to them. They had many laughs together over the amount of news the world had on a virus called Covid and the antidote vaccine that was needed.

Jeez they hadn't even planted their little virus weed yet!

Hacking the IT infrastructure of a Bank or similar was meant to be one of the hardest things to do, impossible hopefully. It was previously part of their job to make it impossible.

In fact, it was as impossible as the whole worlds financial sector collapsing. Once in a 2008 chance!

The flower pot men's little weed was just like Covid. Similar to other viruses but a little more advanced with a few more attachments and ability to morph.

A little sucker of a weed with an electronic brain made of an algorithm that would make Google's search algorithm the possibility of a 5 year old on an IPAD.

Yes their little sucker weed could search and destroy, search and move, search and hide and it carried its own firewall to stop any fire waller attacking it with weed killer.

For two years they had been signing up to as many banks as they could, always utilising on line banking and mobile banking and utilising every single function they could.

They needed a back door and sometimes that door was found through other doors.

For years certain Banks IT security professionals were noticing various attempts, they were used to such, it was their job and their job meant hacker attempts on a regular basis.

With a new little virus weed though, which could break off and leave little bits to grow but doing no harm at that stage, it was possible for these to go undetected. It would appear to the fire waller that the main weed had been eradicated and stoped entirely.

What the twins favourite little weed was doing was simply standing by a door and learning as other bits of data passed through that door and going through the inbuilt security check by the police coding.

Yes, it was internally learning codes and the data structure of all that passed it, a bit like a little memory chip.

At a certain time a little weed they called 'the fertiliser' had to be implanted and before a police code could say "halt or I'll shoot" the weeds would have been activated to open a succession of doors for main little weed to get all the way to the back door but not shut down and stop the bank from working, oh no no no. The bank would work alright and little weed would become big weed with the door firmly shut and some hunky Mexican and Italian mafia electronic door guard codes planted outside.

They knew their fellow professionals would actually be impressed. The twins were impressed too, they never thought they would build such a living code. Block chain had nothing on this little invention.

So now they were ready, they had collated the names of all previous executives of the collapsed banks of 2008.

Also the names of the top people in the then Financial Services Authority and also in the newly named Financial Services Commission. To add a bit of spice, the names of every single MP of the British government (yes that included the Prime Minister – Boris) and all the editors of the newspapers who were about to hear from Domino 2.

Now they did not know who any of the above had accounts with but that was not important, this was an actuary approach, you know 'the chances are type of thinking'.

They were going to attack Barclays, Lloyds TSB and Nationwide.

First Direct was not on their list as they currently banked with them and they thought of them as the most customer focused and ethical bank today.

There was a very good chance that a good number of the above collated persons did have at least one account with one of these banks.

There could be thousands of people with the same name but to ensure they did not cause too many issues to the unintended their little weed that searched simply looked for:-

First Name
Surname
Occupation, if listed
Account Value over £100,000

This way they knew they were only hitting people with money and if any mistaken matches were made there was no great harm.

See, they were not going to steal, they were just going to move and hide. As many of the above mentioned persons, at a certain time, were going to have Zero in their bank balance. Just like the Zero they had in their shares after the collapse.

And as a little bit of fun, they remembered a well learned traveller saying, 'Media has so much impact on all our lives, including ATM machines where everyone reads a message on there nearly every day'.

Well at a certain point in time that message for customers of certain banks was simply going to say "Good Morning, this is Domino 2 – how much money would you like today".

It would say no more than that but that was enough they were sure for customers to be concerned and not conduct any transactions. This would inundate the banks with queries whilst equally wondering, like the whole world would, who the hell is Domino 2.

So the final part of the plan was the communication to the three U.K. papers that they read had received the letter from Domino 1.

Their communication could not be by post nor did they want it to be. Their skill was being invisible in the world of the dark blue yonder, hiding IP addresses and not being traced electronically was a piece of cake.

They had set up a dummy email account ending @whereismymoney.com and they decided the emails to Editors would be sent from domino2@whereismymoney.com

No emails would be sent to any of the other victims that little weed was going to Zero out. No no, the Press could do that.

The email they drafted said:-

Dear Editor,

Firstly we know who Domino1 is *(that was a lie but they thought it added a real extra twist and punch to their message. The only person who knew that was a lie would be Domino 1).*

Secondly, at anytime from now the accounts of any MP, Board Executive of collapsed institutions from 2008, Directors of FSA and FCS and maybe your own accounts will be Zero and the monies removed.

That is if they Bank with Barclays, Lloyds TSB or Nationwide.

This is payback for 2008 financial scandal when nothing was done.

For these accounts to be rectified or for others not to be affected by Domino 2 the following action has to happen:-

1. Your paper must publish this email in tomorrow's or today's tabloid and on line edition. Comments and Like function must be active.

2. You must run an on line customer poll with publication of this email which asks "Do you think that Corporate Corruption should be punished? YES/ NO"

3. You must have a journalist write a feature article about the 2008 collapse. Including why was no one prosecuted?Who made more money when the U.K. government sold off those Banks, that British citizens bought out of solvency, to other banks? Why have those who lost money in shares not been compensated since the value of those companies were

not Zero as the U.K. government used shareholders taxes to keep them solvent and then sold them?

Of course any other investigative work your journalist can do, the better.

You have to release this feature article in the same edition as the feature article you may have chosen to write for Domino 1.

The prize is the release of funds back to where they were and an exclusive interview with Domino 2 on how this was achieved.

Winners will be notified by email. The judges decision is final.

Notes to editors – it is possible for the same virus code to be activated in Banks in the USA and Spain. *(Yes it was possible but the twins had no intention but just like the added connection to Domino 1 they thought this might add more spice to the outbreak of chaos)*

Signing off, yours Domino 2.

Ps. "For evil men and women to succeed it takes good men and women to do nothing".

CHAPTER 8

The Weed is Fertilised

William and Benjamin Mud (*yes I know you could not odds the surname could you*) sat in front of an array of computer screens each connected to each other and all super hacked and untraceable.

They were quite pleased how their email read and were particularly pleased how they were able to connect to another major story from a person they had never met, called Domino 1.

It was 7.00 in the morning and they needed at least 30 minutes after pressing the UPLOAD option to track if their little weed friend had worked. At 7.30 the press SEND button on their email would go.

At 7.30 you could feel an electrifying buzz on all the wiring as SEND was pushed and Domino 2 had fallen.

At 7.33 precisely in the offices of a certain paper called The Daily Digest the feet of a young apprentice named Julie Harper started eagerly dancing under her desk.

Julie always did like the saying "the early bird catches the worm" and she was thankful she always turned up before the other apprentices. Julie was one of those alerted to the auto forward mailbox of any incoming emails to the editor.

Just the FROM email address made her straight blonde hair curl <u>domino2@whereismymoney.com</u>.

Reading the email itself was as electrifying as the current that sent it. Her opening words, not said quietly to herself, were 'oh bloody hell'.

Her first reaction was obvious, change dancing feet to running feet and run to Brad's office.

That morning all the editorial team were in early at Brad's request to catch up on the latest feedback from any other newspapers, police and major social media chatter and comments on the Killer Queen story.

He sat at the end of the table where he could face his glass office door and wall. In mid discussion he could not help but notice a girl flapping her arms holding bits of paper and shuffling her feet dancing. Brad had seen that shuffle before from Julie Harper and he stopped mid flow, as did his heart for a few beats, and ushered her in.

In Julie came, her face lit with excitement and said "you have a message from Domino 2 that you need to read right now".

Without seeing the email the mouths of all 12 sat round the table opened in a gasped shock. Julie had prepared copies already, she was going to prove that an early diligent bird catches the worm. She handed one to Brad first and then one to all the others.

She was excited again simply by the reaction in their faces – this story was biiiiggg, as big as the Killer Queen, if not bigger and the whole Domino story was bigger than both!

Brad was standing and he was not sure if he sat down or fell down in his seat. His first words were "oh my god, what on earth is happening here?"

The other 11 in near unison all said "holy ffffing hell".

"Ok folks, fortune has made this group meet early today, let's take quick stock and again – Julie, you stay please and Bill can you rattle your thoughts first again".

Julie probably had not realised she had already sat down in the chair she had sat down in previously and Brad laughed again inside that her feet were still dancing.

Bill took a minute to intake the content of the email again to be sure he had not missed or misunderstood anything.

He and the others assembled were used to hitting headline stories and calm panic on a daily basis, that was the news business. In all his career though he had never sensed anything as big as this. Before he spoke all that he was about to say and more had quickly rattled through his experienced brain. The one thing that lingered in his silent brain was 'is there a Domino 3 or even more?!'

"Ok", he said, "here are my quick fire, starter for ten, thoughts on the points in the email.

1. "Holy Fuck" and if this is true and people do have zero we need to publish this.
2. "Holy Fuck – over to you Brad – there is no indication Domino 2 has alerted anyone in Parliament. That item is a feature article in itself if they meet as requested.
3. Again, publish the email and we must publish the poll.
4. Probably the second best opportunity received for an investigative journalist within a matter of days.
5. My biggest fear is what if there is a Domino 3 or more?

He could see the sudden realisation and impact on all his esteemed colleagues faces on this last point.

"But my friends what we need to discuss is what is really going on here, I think we all agree that there has been nothing like this in the history of the news. Also we have to validate this, is it a quick copy cat hoax?"

Brad looked a very pale white, not because indeed of the ramification of these 2 dominos and potentially more, but because he had just checked his bank account on his phone – the grand balance of his wealth was £Zero. He now had much more personal interest in how to react to this story and action to take.

The others had noticed that Brad had drifted off into a world of his own and didn't look that healthy all of sudden and even Julie's feet had stopped dancing when she noticed how ill he looked.

"Brad, what's up?" asked Sarah Gough, the political editor for the paper.

"Ladies and Gentlemen, this is no hoax my Barclays account balance is Zero." Instantaneously 11 other people forgot the email and checked their account balances.

Suddenly Julie Harper thought she had better do the same.

One by one they all said "my account is ok"

"Ok folks let's take a breath fill our coffee cups and get ready for the most important session of our lives and use these few minutes to reflect and think more carefully and logically" requested an agitated Brad.

Tea Break 2 for you readers

Hello readers, another tea or coffee or wine break sounds good doesn't it. If you had tea or coffee at the last break I don't suppose you are ready for another. If you chose wine I bet you are on your second glass already and happy to have a third 😊.

I need you to take stock again to help me write this story, this unfolding story can be yours in conjunction with mine.

Remember the Killer Queen story is still in full flow and in nearly every paper. Every paper is reacting differently, each looking for the edge and having their own editorial meetings.

Pay Back project (domino 2) is only just breaking and two other papers may or may not be having the same meetings.

Parliament are not yet aware and only the IT security people and those who have checked bank balances are aware of something but not what. People withdrawing cash are getting a strange ATM machine message. On these last two points alone Social Media is reacting at speed of light again and certainly way ahead of Brad and his team now gathered.

There is an amount of chaos naturally erupting and the breakfast and lunch and dinner chats are rumbling again as many now already know of a Domino 2 as their ATM machine told them and they told their friends anywhere in the world.

So hopefully you can picture the story and the chaos and if you are ready to begin again rejoin me as I follow the route that will show the fate of the dominos.

Thank you.

CHAPTER 9

Coordinated Chaos

"Ok people let's sit down again and discuss what we think the bigger picture is here, away from the individual stories. What do we think the link is between domino 1 and 2? what if there is a Domino 3 with the same sort of request? where do we stop etc? Who has the first opinion?"

From the back of the room a shy little hand went up in the air and a slightly nervous Julie asked "do you mind if I comment?"

"Not at all Julie, the more input the better, this is news at its best and all input is valuable".

"Well" said Julie "I've been monitoring the social media, as you know, on Killer Queen and I see already Domino 2 is known as there are reports of Zero accounts and a strange message from Domino 2 on ATM machines".

The last two comments showed visibly on the faces listening intently to this junior apprentice.

"They are using social media against the media, they

are putting the media on trial or test by enforcing us to deal with subjects we possibly should have done better. By utilising publication of their communications public opinion will impact heavily on how we react.

The youth today hardly read the news any more, they Google stories on subjects that interest them at that time or for facts they need to know. If Google brings up some relevant news stories they might read them. They are not interested in stories of which celebrity bedded who or any of the political in fighting. They will be interested in social media chatter and Memes. I think that whoever the dominos are they are intellectual, mature and are clever enough to try and prove a point. I think that point is that if the press handled serious subjects that mattered the most to people then more people would read the news and then possibly some wrongs corrected."

She ended with "for example" taking the opportunity to vent one of her woes unknown to her sudden audience, "if the media took on a story of the new housing developers and why none are actually affordable by many young families under 35 then it would have interest. They want you to deal with subjects that the public vote to have the most interest on".

Oh it was like Julie had had a crystal ball and knew that Domino 3 was about to topple. What if, in fact, she was Domino 3!

Bill gave Julie a loud round of claps. Appreciation from the oldest in the room to the youngest.

"I totally agree" Bill said "once more they are putting us in the spot light with their sign off 'for evil men and women to succeed it takes good men and women to do nothing' So which camp are we on? I don't think we can take the approach that Domino 1 and 2 are Evil, public opinion would be opposite to that. So they are considered good and they, as well as testing us, are asking for our help and are we good enough to do something?

"This story, if Domino 3 does land, *(yes it will Bill – not to be confused with will kill)* i*s* going to grow maybe to unmanageable levels by any media outlet. We have to react cleverly and go with the flow and speak to our audience in a similar way the Dominos are getting their reaction.

If we write the stories intelligently and understanding enough without committing too much opinion at this stage it will be easier if Domino 3 does fall down.

Brad asked Bill if he had time to write both the feature articles requested from Dominos 1 and 2. His reaction was that he could possibly as both were still close to a 60 day window but that he might not be able to spend as much time in the office and would need Julie full time. The young apprentice was soooo loving being the early worm!

Brad agreed and then summarised the action, in no particular order:-

"Sarah (Gough – Political Editor) you need to make contact with Whitehall and Downing Street and see who has been affected and any press comments yet.

"Simon (surname Rudd / Financial Editor) you are into the banks and their heads of IT. Who has been affected, what are they doing to resolve it? any press statements etc.

"Sandra (Baker – on line and social media editor) You need to publish the email, get the poll going and keep abreast of the best social media fall outs you can. Get some temp staff in if you need to watch the chaos out there.

"Steve (Lark – police and crime Editor) You're onto any and all police contacts across the U.K. and world. Let's get a link between these dominos and let's see what the anti fraud squad think about this.

I'll get the email published and make contact with the other papers to see how the land lays.

And team – I do have to do something about my Zero bank account! This is chaos and it's only going to get worse – regular communication is paramount, there will be enough side stories out of these events to fill the paper for weeks.

So let's co-ordinate the chaos as best we can".

With that they all left at a controlled speedy pace all eager to catch up with the actual chaos that was unfolding out on the streets and the mighty corridors of power in both government and the square mile of London's wealthy Financial Sector.

CHAPTER 9

Uncoordinated Chaos

I t was a Friday morning when the twins Pay Back plan was launched. The most inconvenient day of the week as everyone wanted money for the weekend.

People were noticing longer queues at the ATMs in every town. Not that they were all withdrawing money, it was just that many were standing longer looking at the strange message from Domino 2 and showing it to others nearby.

Many aborted the transaction they were doing in case it was not safe and of those many went into the Bank office to ask what the message was about.

Some, desperate for money, gambled just withdrawing £10 and those that did were greeted with a second message from Domino 2 which said "thank you and remember 'for evil men and women to succeed it takes good men and women to do nothing.'

For the unlucky, relatively few, their machine simply said "there is insufficient funds to be able to complete your transaction – would you like to see your balance?"

Of course such a person was expecting to have a balance of at least £100,000, today it was £00.00. These particular customers, unfortunately for the confused bank clerks, were, to say the least, not happy at all and demanding to see managers whilst other customers inside listened intently to the intense 'complaints'.

Banking staff did not know what to do, the Execs of the banks were not informed, after all they never told their customers they were crashing back in 2008 and they knew for months it was likely. They all knew something was happening now though, that was for sure, at every single branch.

The more astute branch managers took it upon themselves to switch off the ATM's temporarily to await further guidance from Head Office. That didn't help with the internal queues.

After a few hours the frustration of not getting money was growing rapidly and although people could go inside the bank the queues were unimaginable. Also it was coming to the weekend when the banks were shut.

The boardrooms of the three major banks were soon being fully occupied on demand of the CEO's. Heads of IT security were summoned to provide some explanation of what had happened, how it happened, how was it going to be fixed and when?!

....

In 10 Downing Street the Prime Minister and the Chancellor of the Exchequer were already meeting, both having confirmed to each other that they had two separate bank accounts both showing zero.

The rumbles across social media alerted them to a major issue but they were never a recipient of the email sent by Domino 2. Again, the intent was 'how does it feel to have everything gone without being warned and in the power and control of others?'

....

It never actually occurred to the Daily Digest editorial team that the only cc's mentioned were the three papers. No mention at all of copying in the actual banks or members of Parliament.

If they had reflected on this more they would have realised that Domino 2 was putting more pressure on the press to do something more than before, very clever. They had to be the delivery of bad news as well as reporting on the bad news.

Equally, if they had reflected on that thought they would have noticed that they had to question wether it would actually be bad news or seen as great news by the readership masses. After all, it was relatively few who were really affected and of those it was mainly politicians and banking executives.

If Julie Harper had been asked, her quick response would be 'with all the facts seen, to the public it would be great news. Most would see the satisfaction they all would have liked to see back in 2008 – yes for sure, it's great news.'

....

It was not too long before the Prime Ministers' personal secretary interrupted his meeting with the chancellor. She said "I have Sarah Gough from The Daily Digest on the phone asking for your views on the email just received and how many politicians have been affected?"

"What darn email!" came the frustrated response from the PM.

"Exactly my response," she said, adding that Sarah sounded shocked that we had not had a copy sent direct originally. Perhaps we had but it's not made it's way to you yet Prime Minister. She is going to forward it to your private email address I have just given to her assuming that would be ok with you?"

The PM was anxiously opening the email now at the same time as saying "yes of course".

Only after reading the first sentences was the PM mumbling "oh my goodness" repeatedly. He span his monitor around so the Chancellor could read and his face literally painted a thousand words.

His personal assistant, Melanie Carter had seen shocked senior cabinet faces before but she could tell this was something way up on the 'we have an issue scale'.

The PM asked Melanie to call an emergency meeting of the main cabinet and also to be prepared to call an emergency session of Parliament. "Ask, when you speak to any MP if they would check their bank balance too please" he ended.

"After you have contacted the cabinet get me the CEO's of Barclays, Lloyds TSB and Nationwide on the phone urgently – their calls will take priority".

Although he had not been asked for agreement the chancellor was reading the email for the 3rd time whilst constantly nodding and saying "yes, yes" in approval of all the PM had asked for.

Melanie got back to her desk in double quick time and she thought she would get the CEO of Barclays as the first action. He actually would be harder to get hold of later in the day, whereas calling in Cabinet was common and she had a group way of contacting them through many media options.

The contact list of direct numbers for important figures across the U.K. and world held at Downing Street would be a cold callers dream. So it was quite easy for Melanie to call her counterpart Sophie Brook, who was the assistant to Adam Stark CEO of Barclays.

"Hello, this is a call on behalf of the Prime minister, he needs to speak to Adam urgently, as in right now!" was Melanie's polite but well understood request.

Sophie wondered if this was why the executive team were already assembled in Adams office, none of whom seemed to look very happy. Instead of calling through to Adam she gave a knock on his boardroom door and just entered "Adam I have the Prime minister requesting to speak to you right now, I assume you want to take the call?"

"Oh damn – yes you better put the call through"

Adam picked up the boardroom phone to hear "hello please hold for the Prime minister" and then heard the click of the phone being transferred.

He waited for just a few seconds, although today it seemed like an eternity, then heard "Adam, it's Boris, have you had that email from a Domino2? And I assume you are full well aware that something is dreadfully wrong? including the fact that mine and the chancellors accounts with you are showing zero?" "What is happening and when can you come to Downing Street with the CEO of Lloyds and TSB?"

If you needed a description of chaos then today it was written on the face of the CEO of Barclays bank.

"Boris, I have not had any email and no I am not currently aware that any accounts are zero but you have caught me in an emergency meeting with all my executives and security team as we are aware that something on a large scale is wrong".

Before he could add anymore Boris interjected in a more than frustrated tone "bloody hell don't tell me the only people who were informed by email was the damn blooming press! Right you need to see this now, it might speed your meeting up, I'll pass you back to Melanie for your email and she will send it on. When you have read it and discussed with your teams the seriousness and solution to this then call me back urgently and with a time to meet here with cabinet".

"Yes of course said Adam but why the other CEO's?"

"It's all in the email Adam, I've got to go as arranging the Cabinet to come here now".

"Yes of course then Boris, I'll read, talk to my team and be calling you back within the next few hours".

"Ok – bye" was the short closing remark.

Similarly to the Daily Digest team all the executives seated round the boardroom at Barclays were open mouthed and eyes and ears asking questions ten to the dozen but not a word said.

(So my readers, in your tea and wine break did you get to this level of confusion and chaos? If not hang on to your brains because it's going to get worse before it gets better)

Adam read the email and constantly covered his eyes leaning forward and then back in despair with his hands on the back of his head, rocking to and fro and mumbling "no no no".

He shouted to Sophie to quickly print out copies of the email for all in the boardroom and whilst she was doing that he checked his bank balance before re-addressing the anxiously waiting very nervous looking audience.

Once he had seen everyone had read the email he said "right I don't normally swear but what the fucking hell is going on here and how?!". His anger was multiplied not just because he had been called to Downing Street but because his account value was zero and he had many times over £100,000!

His anger could only be slightly comforted that at least it appeared that Lloyds TSB and Nationwide were in the same shitty position. He knew another group call would be needed to be made by him.

"Shannon (Butcher-Jones) you are head of IT security so you have to be first to speak".

"To not mince words Adam this is what the military will say is a real "clusterfuck". Our teams were aware of some kind of cyber attack but we get these attempts all the time.

At around 7.30 this morning our system alerts were telling us a major attack was incoming and our firewalls kicked in as they should and seemed to stop the virus but all of a sudden all the firewalls were opened like a door and some-thing we have never seen before crept in.

It's not like a virus, attacking everything, it's more like a weed only attaching to something it thinks it can grow on or, worst case scenario knows it wants to grow on. Having read the email now I've been running a quick analysis of Zero accounts and it looks as if about 200,000 of our top accounts have been affected".

Adam interjected and said "yes that includes mine and possibly most of yours as well as you are executives of this bank". A couple of hands went up in the air with "mine is ok" and secretly they started thinking about how much does everyone else earn then!

Obviously they all too had checked balances at the same time as reading the email.

The twins would be thinking 'oh yes how important your bank balance is ay, how does it feel?'

"There is mention of USA and Spain, have any of our branches been affected there and why Spain in particular?" delved the ever looking frustrated CEO.

Shannon responded "no signs, not even by social media, that any country other than U.K. affected. I guess Spain as they say this is about 2008 and Santander swallowed up quite a chunk of UK government saved institutions on the cheap but that is only my guess "(*a very good guess Shannon Butcher-Jones*).

Nearly 30 minutes had passed when a knock on the door by Sophie followed by her head leaning in announcing "there is a Peter Butcher-Jones here for Shannon".

"Let him in please, he is my husband and also my top analyst".

'The twins would have been excited, as they knew the Butcher-Jones and had worked on projects for them. The husband and wife team were as good as the twins but unlike the twins they did not lose money or their jobs so they had neither the time or the inclination to give two years birth to a new virus.

Peter Butcher-Jones was quite comfortable that his wife was senior to him and was also his boss. Shannon was far more capable of being political and corporate than he was. He just loved the fact that they both shared the same passion for great coding and IT development. He remembered a time working with a brilliant set of Twins. He always remembered their names as they hated being referred to as 'the flower pot men'.

Peter entered the room and sat next to his wife who had moved a chair in position for him, she gave him a friendly wink as he sat down.

"Before you start Peter I'm just going to see if I can get a conference call now with the CEO's of Lloyds and Nationwide. I suspect they are holding similar meetings and it's time to be partners not competitors". Adam hoped.

He called out to Sophie and said "can you make an urgent call to Tony (CEO Lloyds) and Ellie (CEO Nationwide) and see if you can get them to join as a conference call and patch them through here please".

"On it now" she diligently responded.

"Ok guys let's fill up our coffee cups whilst we see if this conference call can happen, take the time to think more about the issues whilst at at it" Adam encouraged.

(Oooooh we like a coffee and wine time to think don't we readers! So we have the 3 banks meeting, Downing Street in panic with cabinet meeting coming. We still have killer Queen and we have millions upon millions of conversations travelling faster than the speed of light across social media.

There are now two whodunnits and on line social group investigators trying to fathom out who the dominoes are and how are they connected. The police, so far, have a very little part to play and very little they have to go on. Only the traveller could possibly have any potential insight as to who and how and why. Ok coffee cups

*are filled in the boardroom and the phone is ringing –
back to the chaos readers).*

The assembled executives had finished filling their cups,
having just a short time to exchange the odd comment
and thought, and then the conference phone rang. To the
audience it might as well have been an alarm bell.

Adam picked up and said "Tony and Ellie, you both
there?"

"Yes we are here Adam".

He responded "I'm guessing that like me you are all
assembled with your executives in your boardrooms?"

"Roger that" they both surprisingly chose to say in
complete harmony. This made the whole feeling of a war
meeting and maybe it was, trouble is they did not really
know who the enemy was.

"Also like me, have you 1. Had the call from Boris? 2 All
seen the Domino 2 Email? 3 had any decent analysis done
yet?"

Tony said "yes to Boris and Domino, just waiting for our
security analysts to come up soon".

Ellie followed on "exactly the same here Adam, quite a
clusterfuck".

Adam wondered how many times he would hear the
term ' clusterfuck' today and maybe forever and maybe in
the press.

"Ok" he said "my team are all gathered and listening and we are slightly ahead of you in that our top analyst man is about to give his quick overview and I assumed you would want to partner on information and solutions to this?"

"Roger that" came the synchronised reply.

"Ok Peter the floor is yours – no pressure" smiled the CEO.

"Wow, no pressure" Peter commenced with. "Then Adam I assume you don't mind my sharing information about zero accounts?"

"No that's fine provided there is no specific attention to any individual but whilst on here, Tony and Ellie, does Boris Bank with you and is he zerod?"

"Roger to that as well I'm afraid" said the duo

"Carry on Peter" requested Adam again quietly comforted that he was not the the only CEO whose bank had zeroed the prime ministers account.

Peter commenced a little nervously as he knew the immense issue and seriousness of what was unfolding. Equally though from what he had so far seen he was excited as an out and out computer geek.

"Firstly I have to say this is one of the cleverest viruses I have seen. It had to be created by exceptional developers and ones who had a good idea of high security banking protocols. Not only that, it must have taken years but having just read their email that Shannon has showed me about this being payback for 2008 we can assume they've had up to 14 years to think and plan.

Shannon may have told you that this is more like a weed than a virus and being very cleverly selective where it grows and what it not only effects but what it controls.

The good news is that it's actually inactive now, it's not doing anything more, it's has zero'd selective accounts and moved the money but we don't know where yet.

On looking at the zero accounts print out it seems that only those with a value in excess of £100,000, to be accurate £99,999 have been affected. Then only by names matching those execs and politicians mentioned in the email. It was basically a gamble code on matching names hence any unfortunate customer who, say, had £100,000 and was called Boris Johnson then the account was electronically set to Zero.

So the banking system as of now is working as it should. The ATM message was exactly that, just a message, a message to get customers concerned without them really needing to be concerned.

That's is why, if you don't mind me saying, it's so damn clever. They have only affected certain accounts and have accepted the risk of affecting the more well off accidentally but they have actually stolen nothing nor have they stopped us from being operational.

It is easy for us to change the message on the ATM machines. We cannot, at this time, put monies back into the existing accounts as the other clever thing is that we can see there is a system block on any activity on these accounts as if we had cancelled them internally. The other immense clever thing, there is a 60 day time lock on them and it appears that if we wait for 60 days the accounts will go back to normal".

It was a day and time of absolute gobsmacked faces in so many different meetings across the world at the moment. If a photographer could have snapped instantly the faces of all members in all three meetings you would not have seen one different expression.

Adam interjected "Tony, Ellie, do your teams so far have anything to add or comment?"

Ellie said "just wow Adam, I think we can confirm that our systems are working and ATM messages are changeable but not looked at the interruption in code to the level Peter has – well done Peter – excellent she added".

At that time Shannon gave her husband a friendly tap on the knee underneath the table, enabling him to take a breath and sigh. He liked making his wife proud.

Tony added "In short I think that's the same here".

"Tony and Ellie, have you been contacted by the press yet as the email was only sent to them but we have all been contacted by the PM?"

Sophie was still over listening and she interrupted to say "Adam, you have a call to return from Simon Rudd, financial editor of the Daily Digest, he says it is very urgent".

In unison again came a reply down the speaker phone, "I have the same call" said Tony "and me" added Ellie.

"Ok so the one good thing is that we can all control a similar story back to press if you are agreed on that?" Adam was hoping.

"Yes indeed, that would make sense said Ellie but as we are in control I think we should concentrate on a communication to our customers and deal with the Downing Street meeting first and then give more detail for the Press.

In the interim can we get our press secretaries to work on a simple communication to Simon in that we are aware there is something major wrong. That banking systems are still working fine and that, yes, some accounts have been zerod but the money is not lost or stolen and that we are working the best way to put customers back to how they were.

So for 99% of the population banking is as normal and the message in the ATM was a media prank and nothing harmful to their accounts and that such message will or has been removed?

All agreed and Adam concluded the call by summarising:-

1. Ok our press secretaries agree a united response to Simon Rudd.
2. We all correct our ATM messages.
3. Our Marketing teams can separately draw up a communication for us to approve to our customers.
4. I suggest that Shannon and Peter keep in contact with your counterparts and keep on investigating this virus or weed. If we can jointly solve 'where is the money' and a solution that would be great.
5. A priority is for Shannon and your equal teams to identify how to remove this virus and how to stop this from happening again.

And finally, are you both happy to journey to Downing Street together in an hour? If so I'll get in a cab and get them to come pick you both up on the way and we can chat on the journey?"

"Yes seems a good summary and an hour is fine by me" said Tony".

"Me too" finalised Ellie.

"Ok thank you both, see you in about an hour" and Adam ended the call.

"Team, thank you, you all know the work to be done, I should be back from No 10 by 3pm. Call me if anything significant happens or more information is ascertained about how and what etc. We must all meet again in here at

3.30pm sharp." "You all know your roles but until we know more it is business as usual and you must urgently communicate that to all branches and give them a contact here for Zero balance cases.

Shannon and Peter please make sure for Christ sake that the bugger of a virus is really not capable of doing anything more, first sign of more chaos be prepared to shut the entire system down".

All said "yes ok" and speedily left to crack on with the many urgent tasks to be undertaken.

CHAPTER 10

Meanwhile, elsewhere

Meanwhile, whilst chaos was erupting (by the minute and hour), the twins were diligently watching the success of Pay Back on their computer screens. They were amazed at the flow of social media chat already brewing. So many posts with 'I went to the cash machine and this is the message I got' with attached photo of said screen saying 'welcome from Domino 2'.

It was the amount of 'me too comments' in reply to various threads from all over the country that made the boys smile at their handy work.

There were also a few who had posted 'i proceeded with a £10.00 withdrawal as wasn't sure it was safe and this is the second message I got' photo of ATM screen uploaded of "for evil men and women to succeed it takes good men and women to do nothing".

The most fascinating thing was a growing number of posts that responded to these particular messages saying 'ooooh I went back and tried that, actually got £20,00 ok and I did get that message too.'

And as the day was to roll on the traffic just constantly increased. Not one person posted, so far, 'I went to get some money and it said my account was zero.'

The twins actually didn't need any more publicity and they wasn't really that bothered if any of their requests were followed. They could see already their core objective had been achieved. They knew the public would get to know why they did this even if their email was not published.

No person in need had been caused any loss, the banks could still operate and those with Zero accounts would, at some point, get their money showing again.

....

In Africa Sonia Parker was aware of a couple of people who had posted they had Zero in their bank accounts. They were American Trophy hunters living in England and had posted on the Will Kill group site asking if people thought this might be connected to Domino 1.

Sonia had kept reading thousands of posts and although the email had not yet been published both the ATM messages made her aware that there was now a Domino 2.

So she assumed someone at least did understand her

sign off. Who that was she didn't know or why? Could it be the traveller she wondered?

What she did know is that she had no contact from the police and all she could see from continued press stories was that there was no idea who shot Tanya Wild and hence who Domino 1 was.

She too was not bothered if her feature article was printed or not. Thanks to a discussion with a kind traveller the media had done its job already and the public will decide if good men and women had taken sufficient action.

Bill Cartwright would have been impressed with his summary of what might be part of the bigger picture.

....

Elsewhere back in England a rather frustrated individual had been mesmerised by the two main social media stories taking place. The strange link of Domino 1 and 2 was becoming the biggest mystery and whodunnit.

They had the urge, just like the twins, to implement a plan. In that plan, media attention, all they now needed to do is call and say 'hello this is Domino 3 and I would like to speak to the Editor.'

....

Somewhere, continuing his travels although limited because of Covid, a well travelled gentleman had noticed on his one and only social media account the Domino stories.

It was only he who could know who Domino 1 and 2 might be, certainly not sure, but certainly a good idea and not only that he might have pictures.

If Domino 3 and more were to surface this traveller might be the only person who had a solution. Amongst continuing to rattle the worlds issues over and over in his constantly thinking brain and how such worlds issues could be solved, he was now reflecting too on how he would solve the Dominos from cascading further.

CHAPTER 11

Politics

The three Banking CEO's arrived at 10 Downing Street a couple of hours after their conference call having had chance to get updates from all their teams on the action points.

ATM messages had been changed with no sign of any reaction from 'the weed'. They all had opened a new account in the exact name of Boris Johnson – occupation politician – amount £100,001 – (to be sure). Nothing prevented this account and again there was no unusual code activity to remove the funds.

All teams had tried to conduct various actions on the Zeroed accounts but to no avail. It was a bit like Jurassic Park when the programmer created a pop up of 'ah ah – you cannot do that' except it just said 'illegal operation' in a line of code and not an actual message.

The more astute developers knew the sarcastic point of that message and had to grin.

No one had yet discovered where the moved money had gone. It appeared one Ghost Account had been created at each Bank and then all of them made invisible as if coded with invisible ink. So they were there but could not be seen without the correct filter or dye. If this was true though it meant that a solution would be easy.

They could all get reports on how much went missing and who from so there was always a solution eventually. The issue was not just missing funds for withdrawal though it meant direct debits and other payments would fail. The twins knew this and thought that was a minor bit of inconvenience for those who were at fault compared to the "inconvenience" of loss of homes and savings and jobs to those in 2008.

It was equally a minor inconvenience to those who were innocently affected. The twins could live with that.

Customer communications were written and the agreed holding release to Simon Rudd and other newspapers had been issued.

The three CEOs were as pleased as they possibly could be with the action taken. Adam tried adding some comfort by saying "At least we were not CEOs of any bank that collapsed in 2008 and that was far far worse than this".

As his words finished leaving his mouth all three realised he had said exactly what Domino 2 was trying to say. They had just unwittingly convicted their previous peers of a very serious crime. Those crimes went unpunished, the fate of these three, as final gatekeepers to customer security, was yet unknown.

They were shown into the Cabinet office as soon as they arrived. From the list of prepared Zero accounts they had, sorted by occupation and names they knew before arrival that everyone in that room, as far as their banks were concerned, were worth nothing.

Adam took lead speaker again and presented everything that had been raised in their conference meeting.

They explained that they were operating as normal and just had to solve how to get Zero accounts operational but that it looked, for speed, that new accounts might have to be manually opened and credited with the amount last held plus any interest. All standing orders and direct debits would also have to be replicated.

The Cabinet, much to the delight of the three anxious bankers, seemed relieved but such relief was with the warning Adam gave to his team 'you better bloody well be sure this virus is still not active and can do anymore damage'.

One additional point "have your security teams contacted Scotland Yards Cyber Crimes team?" We need to be able to try and catch the culprits of this sooner rather than later" challenged the PM.

Although all three had forgotten to discuss this in view of the chaos, Adam responded "our three security teams are in liaison and will be contacting them soon once more information can be documented for the crimes unit". Tony and Ellie nodded in unknown agreement.

Boris thanked the three for their speedy action and attendance and asked them to stay whilst the Cabinet dealt with something that was now their main responsibility. That was whether to announce that parliament would be asked to discuss a new law dealing with corporate corruption or negligence and imposing a mandatory jail sentence if convicted.

He started "once the press have published the email all the other media will be immediately asking for a response from No 10's press office including TV. It was best that Central Government took a lead in communications as this event was now of National interest and importance".

The PM said "we have an opportunity to be pre-prepared and would be most interested in our guests opinions on such a point. Particularly as the press would be speaking to them and asking if this event was gross negligence". (*Ooooh the twins would love to be a fly on the wall for that answer*)

The cabinet members had be shown a copy of the email sent to the press. An email the PM had been advised by the press would be published that night or in the morning. It was likely to be in the online media that night in view of the fact social media had already circulated widely and it was best the public started to know the full facts.

Addressing the Cabinet the PM said, "my colleagues, we need to take stock of a slightly bigger picture here first. I think our Banking CEO's have given us sufficient information to ride the storm of another banking crisis. The hotline being set up for zero account holders will be the most important to resolve anyone of influence fuelling the political cauldron.

What I would first like to discuss is this so called Domino 1 and 2. The event in Africa has not really affected us as the U.K. but now we have the Domino 2 event in our territory many will be trying to make a connection.

In addition, in both events, only the press have been communicated with and in both communications there seems to be the aim of bringing senior individuals and politicians to task on each featured subject. And, is there a domino 3? I am concerned about that!

I think we should ask Scotland Yard to make more enquiries of the Trophy Hunt killing in case they find anything about their culprit that connects them to our cyber culprits.

Then we need to decide should we give into such demands and if we do will it be seen as giving into terrorists?"

'If Bill Cartwright and Julie Harper had been sitting in this meeting they would have slumped their heads into their hands in disbelief as to how they (MP's) simply did not understand'

Fortunately for the PM the youngest minister, Ann Drake, had a number of qualifications in psychology and was quick and brave enough to immediately respond with some indignant thoughts.

"Prime minister I think you are missing the big and intended picture here. The press are being used as not just a voice but as investigators to make the public the judge and jury. It seems to me that whoever the Dominos are they are indeed very clever. Public opinion is already on their side, they will know that you, at least, have been asked to announce that you will, at least, and I emphasise, at least ask Parliament to discuss such a law.

Equally they are asking the public to consider who is evil and which good people do nothing. Their whole point seems to be is that they want people to find a conscience and challenge 'did we do enough'?

How we react now will be gauged against how we reacted back in 2008 and when I say 'we' I mean the entire parliament. I would classify that the correct response is possibly an election winning one".

At this point the audiences attention could be seen to visibly change.

Ann continued "One point in our particular favour is that it was Labour who was in charge in the collapse in 2008. We have to simply be intelligent in our press releases and communications. In fact, I would go one step further and say we need to be actively seen as willing to help the journalists write their feature article unless of course anyone in this room thinks we have anything to hide from past or future.

The way we react now potentially could minimise any chance or impact of a domino 3."

The PM was quite taken aback by the response, mainly because it did make actual sense. In a way he thought to himself the dominos were saying 'things cannot carry on as before, more wrongs need to punished, they have to change and good people have to step up and make a true difference. 'Not do nothing' the penny dropped in the PM's brain.

As the PM came out of his own thoughts he decided he would put his three banking guests on the spot.

"Adam, Tony, Ellie, you are bound to be contacted by the press on your thoughts on this bearing in mind the accusation is that some of your earlier peers should be imprisoned. In fact they might even try and liken this event to such?"

The three CEO's were already whizzing this over in their brains as soon as the PM had announced the discussion to be had. All three had reflected on the innocent comment in the taxi 'not as bad as those in charge in 2008'. Equally as unsaid as the other thoughts they had rationalised that no one had actually lost any money so no court of law would count them as being grossly negligent.

This time it was Ellie who took the lead in speaking.

She said "although events over the past few days have not given much time to think, in what we have had I believe many of us have had our conscience telling us to take a step back and think more like and for the Dominos. So I agree with much of what Ann has just said".

So for example, if I myself had lost all my money and it was not my fault and such money was meant to be protected by a Government oversight body (FSA) and by highly paid people at that – my public head would immediately say "yes". Not just Yes but that Parliament should be the ones knowing such laws should be created and not forced to think by agitated citizens.

Without fear of known punishment corporate negligence crimes are easy to get away with.

As a CEO am I worried that this is how my thoughts are? yes of course I am but the important thing is what is the right thing to do? I think there is danger all round in dominos continuing and public outcry if the action on any of the points is 'to do nothing'.

So I agree that you should at least announce that it will be discussed in parliament. That is all they asked for and as a member of the public if the shoe was on the other foot I would be voting in favour.

I'm sure, that like myself, my two colleagues are certain of their abilities to operate their ship effectively. The 2008 collapse could have been prevented, that is a fact.

Provided there are sensible guides drawn to classify what entails corporate corruption and negligence these can be incorporated in all Companies KPI (key performance indicators) and as an agenda item on every board and shareholder meeting.

If then such events happen breaking the laws then someone is obviously negligent or criminal and should be held accountable. Please note though, I am assuming that one of the guidelines will be that there must be a significant loss to be held accountable against and not just any frustrated agitator.

A round of applause came from Ann Duke and a humble but agreed expression from Adam and Tony.

Ann chipped in "exactly, the penny is dropping, the dominos are not saying that everyone in their target categories are evil, they are potentially saying that they are good but just did nothing".

She also added "my learned CEO's it's not for me to advise you but if you can recall Ellie's words I would use that response to any approaches from Press along with your updates on the Domino 2 event. As a customer of yours that is the exact response I would want to hear".

All around the table, consciences were being challenged by their brains, the penny was dropping, they had to decide were they a part of anything evil (corruption would be considered more evil than good) or were they just guilty of doing nothing or not enough?

It was the PM who closed the session actually feeling

relieved that Ellie had probably come up with the perfect approach to not just this but many things in parliament.

He said "I think that is excellent" I'm going to announce that parliament will meet and I'm calling parliament to sit now to update them on this particular banking issue and of the decisions here today".

"I want to thank you all for your attendance and my parting request to our three guests is that please come back urgently with the actual solution to these Zeroed accounts as I'm sure a great number of other MP's will be in the same position".

The three agreed and left to get the same taxi together to continue their CEO chats in an eager journey to rejoin their awaiting teams in the boardroom.

The Cabinet all departed to a not too far away drinks cabinet.

CHAPTER 12

Faster than light

That evening the three newspapers broke the story on-line and by the following morning every newspaper had been able to make it a front page headline. Only three papers were able to say they had received the letters directly.

Headlines consisted of:-

"Another banking crisis looms" (*those in the know thought . . . why?! Not the banks CEO's nor parliament would consider this a crisis.*

"Where is your Money" (*that was quite clever and amusing based on the domino2@whereisthemoney.com and a question everyone wanted the answer to.*

"Trophy Hunting and Finance – Is there a connection?" (*Was a more deep thinking inside page headline*)

"Another Domino falls – is there a Domino 3" (*taking a different route than the others based on the amount of social traffic by on line investigators. The editorial team here trying to get readership as they were not a main recipient of the email.*

The one headline which caused the most eye attention was one which played on the conscience of every citizen. It simply said:-

> *"For Evil Men and Women to Succeed it takes Good Men and Women to do Nothing".*

That was the headline of the Daily Digest and that was thanks to Bill and Julie. Their whole story lines on all dominos will be gauging their own conscience in front of their readership challenging 'was enough done and will enough be done now and in the future'.

That edition of their paper was their highest selling to date.

The news spread through every computer, radio wave and cable possible.

Around many breakfast, lunch and dinner tables the Dominos were being questioned and judged. The common question being asked by these volunteer jurors (billions of them now by the way) was:-

'What would you do if you were Domino 3?'

Unfortunately for the press and parliaments around the world the various options for any Domino 3 would have made more headlines than I would have time to write.

Only one person knew what Domino 3 would do and they were pleased that they had many others who would agree with them by reading their comments to the above question.

CHAPTER 13

Back in Africa

*We must not forget Africa my readers as the Killer Queen
story is still bigger out there and in other countries than
the U.K. banking issue and the link to Domino 2 is
making it stay that way.*

Back in Africa Sonia Parker sat in her very humble
small home. She had read The Daily Digest headline on line and it's subsequent story along with
many others.

In front of her was a picture of Sam and Naomi with the
greatest of smiles on their faces and a huge giraffe leaning
over Naomi.

Underneath this picture she had hung a piece of tree on
which she had hand carved:-

*For Sam and Naomi – "For evil men and
women to succeed it takes good men
and women to do nothing"*

It would take the smartest of investigators to ever realise that might ever be the only clue given by Domino 1, at that time, as to a possibility of her identity.

The South African Parliament had been in communication with the other African Parliaments to see if there were any other Trophy Hunter type attacks at any time in the past few months. Also to discuss joint opinions if approached by the Press on the feature articles to be written.

The 'where has the money gone' in the U.K. Domino 2 event might become a second accidental link to the two events.

Everything was always about money and many people dreaded the questions about 'where has all the money gone.'

The Africa Nations were always concerned that tourism of real animal lovers to their wonderful reserves was more important than trophy hunting. Not just their whole economy but also for the local tribes and villages that survived in the traditional way by selling hand made ornaments and other goods to the welcome visitors.

The growing number of complaints from these visitors, when they heard that private hunting was going on in the same reserves they were visiting, had not gone unnoticed.

Adding in the fact of the dwindling population of all feline species was indeed making trophy hunting an issue of a size they might not want to admit.

A member of the Zimbabwe Government recalled a really interesting talk he had with a friendly, knowledgeable western traveller. The traveller listened well to issues and was quickly able to suggest things which should be a simple solution. The 'but' was because either people never tried or there was corruption and greed somewhere preventing action.

The traveller had said 'Africa needs to realise that it is the guardians of mother earths most precious creatures on behalf of all the world. Your animals are not found anywhere else and yet the world wants you to protect them. For that there should be a greater plan and for that a cost. That cost for the worlds governments would be insignificant but it would dwarf the income Africa receives from Trophy Hunting.

The government minister was so enthralled by the simplicity but understood exactly the inference that it was politics and politicians themselves who never really had the inclination to solve it. That aside he still shared a number of beers over a dinner and listened to what such a plan for Africa would look like.

He thought that might be a good thing for him to talk to the press about.

'And while you were reading this chapter readers a few more million posts and comments have been made in the continuing episodes '

CHAPTER 14

Back in the U.K.

t's the day after the Domino 2 story broke in media everywhere. The Daily Digest editorial team had agreed to meet an hour earlier every day (for those possible) as there was so much to catch up on. Julie Harper was invited and she had no problems with that at all (early bird catches worm).

The only person missing was Bill Cartwright as he had to take time out to plot his approach to two very different feature articles. Also plan to whom he would want to speak to and how. His task was going to be made slightly easier once, via Sarah Gough (political editor) and Simon Rudd (Financial Editor), he had contact with Ann Drake (cabinet minister) and Ellie Fowler (CEO Nationwide).

Adam asked Sandra (Baker – on line editor) what the result of the poll was published both on-line and with a link in the main tabloid for readers to participate. She responded "this was the most active Poll we have ever ran and it's 80% in favour of a new law" over 1,000,000 people, so far, took part."

'I emphasise again readers. All the papers are meeting and even radio stations and tv shows ran the poll'

"Crikey" was the best word Adam could think of. "And Julie how would you summarise general social chatter on both stories?"

"Relentless" was her best word. She added "wow talk about stir public interest, this must be doing all media a favour in sales".

Adam chipped in "yes folks our edition yesterday with the headline from Bill was by far our best seller".

Julie said, "there is an immense amount of chatter about which papers will write the feature articles or not. Even more chatter and an immense intrigue on whether the dominos will really reveal themselves to the winner and if so would they both come together, whoever they are!". Julie added, "I think that whenever that edition comes out for any paper that will be their best sales day".

All attendees looked at each other and then to Bills empty chair.

"Ok, so all good as far as we are concerned. Sarah and Simon, how are you getting on with Downing Street and CEO bank contacts?" Both responded that they had managed to arrange meetings today after receiving what were obvious jointly produced holding releases.

"That's good, the whole of the U.K. is now aware that Boris announced his plan to hold parliament to discuss the new law and maybe we should pass on our Poll stats and overview of social media activity".

They all agreed and the meeting was kept as short as possible as they did have other stories to catch up on. If every one of them were honest though these domino stories had reignited a dormant journalistic nature in them.

The public were massively interested and they were being forced to the Press to look for some very good answers to a number of very good questions.

At that time they were pleased Bill had not retired as his journalistic candle had never blown out. He was old school and his approach with the "For evil men etc" headline was brilliant.

The fact that their youngest attribute was also showing immense talent meant they covered the age spectrum from 20 to 64.

When Domino 3 falls they will be glad of such a wide spectrum.

Domino 3 was going to literally hit many homes.

CHAPTER 15

Unity not division

The Dominos were not really sure how much they would achieve. For both it was an urge to push a gamble that they would be heard. Be heard by the right good people who could and should do something.

It was not even Sonia Parker's intention to kill. She was only going to wound Tanya and frighten the majestic lion away. At the point of having Tanya in her sights though all she heard was the screams of dolphins only out screamed by those of her daughter. The message she saw was 'it's only dolphins'. That was the cue for Sonia's demon to take over the trigger and that demon said 'no it isn't it's my beautiful daughter – take that you fucking evil bitch'. And her sight adjusted from shoulder to head in a nano second.

When Sarah got through to Downing Street again she was surprised that she was met with some readiness. In fact they said the cabinet had nominated Ann Drake to speak to the press on their behalf including, of course, the PM.

Simon hit equal luck when he called back to chase the three CEOS and it was Ellie Fowler who called back. She said "I need to give you apologies on behalf of Adam, Tony and myself, as you can imagine it's been a hectic couple of days and solving the issue was more important than talking about it. The three of us travelled together to Downing Street and agreed I could be the lovely lady to speak to Press. I can talk about issues affecting all the banks but of course I cannot comment on any individual banks own issues and workings other than mine, is that ok?"

Simon was taken aback somewhat and said "yes that's perfect, are you able to talk about views on the Cabinet being asked to discuss a new law?"

"Yes indeed we are united on a response to that".

.... "Hello, Simon are you still there?"

"Sorry yes, I was just quickly thinking, that is perfect" *(Simon wasn't thinking, he was stunned into silence)*

That was not to be the end of stunned silence when Ellie then added, "in fact Simon, I agreed with Ann Drake that we would meet Press together if need be and I know she is speaking to your colleague Sarah Gough, is that correct?"

"Yes it is and that is really brilliant" Simon knew he said in a bewildered tone.

"Ok great, well I'll liaise with Ann and get her PA to call you back with the hope of, if you are ok, meeting up tonight over a light dinner. We all have priorities on and we good people have to invest even more of our daytime I guess to get things done".

Simon knew now she had read Bills full headline story under "For evil men and woman to succeed it takes good men and women to do nothing" Good old journalist Bill he thought – good honest journalism opens doors *(yes but not as sneakily as Bill and Bens little weed did to get you here in the first place)*.

The call ended and a meeting was arranged that night.

What was a surprise to both Ann and Ellie is that after their Downing Street first meeting they arranged for a really early 6am breakfast together as they were fascinated by each other's like-minded contribution.

They were amazed that they discovered they both had a side passion for endangered animals and both, a few years back, (before their current positions) had worked on the same Orangutang Sanctuary in Indonesia for ten days but not at the same time.

However, they had both met this other traveller who was there for 30 days.

They recalled how he had listened a lot and then came up with some enlightening remarks. He was not just well travelled but quite learned on many things, including highly paid jobs in the financial world. He seemed to have solutions in his head to many things that bothered many people.

They both recall he said something along the lines:-

.

'the trouble is that people won't admit they are wrong, the higher position the less wrong they are. Then meetings of equally high people defend the wrong creating a chain of wrongs that can last for years. When eventually someone tries to correct the issue it's grown so far on from what caused the first wrong that they forget they have to go all the way back to the beginning to correct issues.

Ego's, profits and protecting of ones territory in the Corporate and other sectors and lack of co-operation by the right and good people is probably the cause of all issues. Solve that and you can solve any issues.'

'Including solving the extinction of Orang-utans and Sun Bears' he had added with a wink, they both recall, as he had left them to their wine.

And . . . his parting comment to both was "for evil men and woman to succeed it takes good men and women to do nothing".

Although the dominos were not really sure what they would achieve if they knew their goal was a long way forward already they would be smiling.

Ann, Ellie, Sarah and Simon were going to meet and sometime in that meeting they were going to admit some wrongs.

CHAPTER 16

Domino 3
Felicity Myers

Dear readers, it's not another break. I need to let you know I'm changing my writing style for this Domino. This is a lovely woman at her wits end and she has had enough. The best way I can write this is by rambling – I'm sure you can get into her head and then I'm sure you can hear her shout and rant all this . . . so for a while become Felicity Myers as she lets rip – oh boy does she let rip – let off steam with her, I'm sure millions can relate.

Felicity Myers was a real, down to earth, god send to the earth. She was not only just a brilliant, funny caring hardworking mum *(that is actually her children's words not mine)* but she was sensitive and caring to all around her.

She was also an Earth mother and loved all animals.

A lady not really one for social gossip and she loved her country recluse away from crowds. However, whoever she met liked her *(except maybe her MP and town planners – see below).*

Felicity Myers had a few demons though that were growing and had been growing for nearly two years now.

Her tranquility was being disturbed. By *imbeciles she would want me to add.*

You see, her country recluse was becoming not a country recluse but a huge bloody town. No, she can't say town as a town indicates, doctors, dentists, shops, schools, playgrounds and much more. No, no, no her country recluse was basically just becoming a mass of housing developments looking like one whole development. Toy towns where governments filled them from the supply of humans in the Matrix causing chaos to everyone.

The order had come down from Government, the Council would say, that we have to build more houses they said.

That seemed strange to Felicity as no one she had spoken to in her town had ever said they were short of houses and all the estate agents had full property books and windows displays.

She and thousands of others complained and tried to input into what was called the local development plan. A plan that was meant to drive development and basically have all input listened to by the Council and include an infrastructure resembling some normality of human life.

All that happened was is that the usual large developers got their way and farmland became massive, seen your houses before, housing estates.

The few country roads became chaos, the two dentists, one doctors, one comprehensive school were full before the new houses were even built! Her youngest child was now actually refused a place in the same secondary school as their sibling because it was impossible to take anymore children. This meant a 45 minute bus ride to the next town where she might find herself lucky to get a place because that bigger town was having even bigger housing estates built!

She was also a horse rider and the Council had said they don't like Bridleways. 'It's a bloody rural town where people bought homes to escape and ride bikes and walk and cycle and have horses!' (Grrrrrrr)

All these rural pastimes are surely part of the modern demand for diversity, surely. But No no no no no no People were leaving the city, driving too bloody fast on country roads and moaning at the dog walkers, horse riders and hikers who were on the country roads. 'Yes on the country roads way before you arrived matey ' Felicity would curse often when she heard of such complaints.

Her tranquil life was no longer tranquil and she was angry at how angry she was at stupid unintellectual politicians, councillors and planners.

She wrote to her MP who was basically of no use at all as she realised that no MP had any power over any local decision. None, none at all – just voted in by the party someone wanted to vote for without any knowledge of who or what this elected person could do for them. They were basically just an inbox for whatever front line minister was in charge of the issue.

Felicity decided to meet said MP and let him have some good old fashioned motherly love and pointed out to the MP "do you know that because the new home house buyers cannot get their kids into school or doctors or dentists that they are not that happy)She did also think what idiots these people were to buy homes not checking on such facilities first) . . . And do you know that probably 80% of the existing community are not happy. And by the way, do you know that none of the hardworking youngsters in this town can afford any of the bloody homes that have been built. And do you know how many millions of pounds profit these developers have made along with the landowners and put no infrastructure in and left this town in misery.

And where are all the new council taxes going ay? The millions of pounds the council are getting from these thousands of new homes? To the councillors and politicians bloody pay rises I bet!

Yes this town is left in god damn bloody misery and it's your constituency and you want us to vote for you but all you can do is say 'you'll take my complaint up with the housing minister and Secretary of State!!!'.

No that's no bloody good, you need to stop the housing minister and Secretary of State being so bloody stupid and actually tell Councils how to plan before they build. And if enough of this community insist you SHOULD have the power to stop any work until we are satisfied with plans! What is the point of a local development plan otherwise!

There is not one planner in any planning department across the entire bloody country – they are just the decision makers on who gets permission to build and that's it!

If you plan that means you draw up a whole area of the Town or even County if you like. You mark where and why you want more houses you mark where roads are needed, you put in schools and doctors and dentists and hospitals, maybe even longer train platforms, and vets and then you plan and plan! The Council spends the money on an architect to draw up a vision not just for the unqualified councillors but for the whole community to see and comment.

Then and only then! do you ask landowners to tender their land and developers to draw plans and tender for the work. Not apply and win per site like now. That tender has to include how they will finance and build the infrastructure instead of ruining all our lives and walking away to their lovely untouched recluse with millions and millions of pounds!!!

It's all bloody nonsense and chaos – a planner is meant to co-ordinate and plan to stop chaos – and you can't do anything but pass this on as a complaint!!! Well pass it bloody well on then you can't do anything idiot!

And another thing actually, I'm not finished now, so many bloody large construction vehicles every day on roads not built to take them. These are ruining the roads and it will be us council tax payers picking up the bill, not the damn rich developers. Annnnd while I'm on a roll, they are closing and restricting council dumps to families and all sorts and then you wonder why there is fly tipping also ruining our countryside!! It could not get any more ridiculous and all those in charge need firing or shot!! Pass that on as well!

As you can tell readers Felicity was not happy – did you catch her mood and have a vent?

Well, there is more to Felicity. She has her own plan, she saw a great headline about "for evil men and women to succeed it takes good men and woman to do nothing".

This level of incompetence in government, councils and planners was Evil, might be unintentional Evil but it certainly wasn't good. She felt it was evil – 45 bloody minutes to take my next child to another school. It was stupid evil!

Too damn right, bloody MP and planners did nothing and they know that 80% of the population of affected areas are unhappy – they know about the schools and doctors and roads. They are not going to stop and admit they are wrong as they should have done a couple of years ago – oh no they are not going to stop they are going to actually build even more houses!

Well time I stopped doing nothing!

CHAPTER 17

Domino 3
The Plan

Felicity did not get where she was today without being smart, oh no. Smartest mother and wife every side of her MP for sure.

The urge to do something was actually making her smarter and she reflected on a lovely down to earth guy she met on her travels. Hers were not travels of a lonesome world, need to escape, kind though. She was on a family holiday but took a day out for herself to walk up the mountains. That is where she met this traveller having lunch out of his ruck sack on the top of the highest peak.

She too had packed a, top of the mountain, lunch and it was a cracking view and a common thing for sole mountain hikers to join each other at the top of any getaway. Felicity got into a flow of chatter quite comfortably and it was not long before she explained the annoyance of 'planning'.

Her newly found, top of the mountain, mate seemed to calmly understand and could easily rattle off more than she. Even the amounts actually kept by councils in an old building clause which meant developers had to leave so much in an infrastructure fund. The developers chose to do this readily rather than build as the latter was too time consuming and costly. The councils however did nothing with this fund!

Well, she immediately thought then how her rant with her MP could have gone on a little longer.

Anyhow, this man had simply said ' if the local press and national press were to unite on such issues they would have massive support and hence more readership for a while. I think at some point an event will happen and a domino effect will fall on the untold story. That is that there is no actual planning and that follow the money and where does it all go will be an eye opener causing uproar'.

In parting she remembered how he even said "for evil men and women to succeed it takes good men and women to do nothing".

For her plan, she bought, believe it or not folks, a burner phone! She learned about these from crime movies.

Whilst she was thinking that she was likely to become Domino 3 a thought occurred to her. What if her mountain friend was actually one of the Dominos, what if he in fact was both of them!

She held that thought and looked up the phone number of the Daily Digest (as she liked their story) and called and said "Hello is the editor there please I have an urgent story for him"

"May I ask who is calling please?"

"No I'm sorry I cannot tell you, I need to tell him"

"He never really takes any unknown calls directly madam"

"Well you need to tell him that I know who the dominos are then and if he wants to know he has to take this call right now and have a large bit of paper handy or he can record the call, I don't care, but you have one minute from now".

"Hold on a second please" tick tick tick tick. . . .

"Hello this is Brad Stevens Editor – you have some wanted news I gather about the dominos?"

"Brad, yes you need to listen carefully and be quick. I do know who the Dominos are because my main important message is that I am Domino 3 and I have some instructions for you – are you ready now?"

The poor Editor found himself in another state of stunned silence but managed to blurt out after a few seconds "I'm listening intently".

"Unlike the other dominos I've not actually done anything yet, we actually don't want to cause more harm if we have to, but what will happen is that on November the 5th a, very likely to succeed, attempt to blow up the Houses of Parliament will happen. We want to make sure the building is empty as the sight of the parliament being destroyed will be enough. You only have to think how easy it is for crop dusters to fly across to London Brad.

Now have you that pen and paper handy? Your papers task is that I want your journalist Bill Cartwright to write a feature article on the disastrous impact on families, especially rural families), of the massive housing developments going on across this country. It must include:-

1. Where are the affordable houses for youth?
2. Where is the infrastructure plan for roads, schools, doctors and dentists etc?
3. Why are bridleways in rural towns considered a nuisance by rural councils?
4. How many millions do developers make?
5. Why do council planners not produce a complete plan?
6. This is a request from Domino 2 – where has all the money in council taxes, planning fees and developers infrastructure fund gone?

And Brad, as usual, any additional investigative input, name and shame would be great, you know brown envelope development and all that.

Article to be released at same time as the other two Domino articles.

Judges decision will be final.

And do you know what your Prize is Brad?

Brad interjected for the first time "a meeting with you?"

Yes, but better than that Brad, Bill Cartwright gets to meet me as soon as you have published, in full, details of the information from this phone call but it must be published tomorrow as I need a bit of time for me bomb making. Once I see it published I will make contact with Bill to arrange the meeting and then his feature article can include me but nothing about Domino 1 and 2. Their competitions are theirs.

Have you got all that Brad?"

"Yes" he said, "I recorded the call".

"I thought you might, good lad and be jesys Brad, remember now won't you "for evil men and woman to succeed it takes good men and women to do nothing".

With that she ended the call abruptly and was pleased she could now lose the strong Irish accent that she was very good at. She could also lose the burner phone which really made her feel like part of a thriller movie.

Brad ended the call with a glass of whiskey that he had not had the need to do in such a long time.

CHAPTER 18

Clever Lady Ay

Well I don't know about you readers but I'm impressed with our Felicity, aren't you?

She was just building on what Domino 2 did. She lied and said she knew the Dominos.

Her way of getting her story published was not by the threat but by actually offering a journalist to meet Domino 3 who knew Domino1 and 2.

Plus she used "WE didn't want to hurt" and put the other two dominos in a good light with the middle of the road commentators. Dominos 1 and 2 would really like Felicity if they did know each other (one day, another chapter maybe)

And to help Domino 2 she linked them to the possible financial corruption of planning – finance stuff was Domino's 2 little bug bear.

Not only that, she put in a great Irish accent and made up a thought about flying a Dust Cropper plane into the Houses of Parliament and then a joke from an Irish lady about needing to make a bomb.

You have to take off your hat to this 'right for her fight for a life" lady don't you.

Young Julie Harper, if you thought she danced a lot she would be able to perform in Riverdance once she hears about this. And she will in just a short while!

And readers I don't know about you but even I need a glass of wine now and I'm writing this story.

Crumbs the public are going to love this aren't they.

The gossip on this one is going to be far worse than Guy Fawkes actually succeeding on November the 5th 1605. I'm sure the press will write that they are surprised it's taken over 600 years for such another attempt.

Hope your brain is keeping the chaos momentum going as even I'm losing where the chaos has got to so far.

I wonder if your story is better than mine?

Now on with the show . . .

CHAPTER 19

Dinner o'clock

Brad was a really calm organised editor used to daily deadlines and breaking stories and change of column, stories and headlines etc.

As he finished asking his PA (Lucy Game) to assemble the editorial team again, if they were in, he for the first time felt unable to be as logical and co-ordinated as possible.

Domino bloody 3 and the chance to meet them, know who domino 1 and 2 are . . ., destroy Houses of Parliament . . . and yet and yet bloody yet he understood the Irish lady. His town were in uproar over development and he thought he could write this requested feature article without Bill.

And then . . . another penny dropped on a character in this story . . ., why had he not done so before! He would call himself a good man and he knew the anger all his neighbourhood friends felt but he never thought of it as a National major public story, not in the way he suddenly knew how his Irish lady wanted it covered.

Well this Irish lady, Domino 3, certainly had enough rationale to blow up Parliament.

Anyhow readers I need to come back to this meeting as just introducing this so you know that Sarah and Simon are now aware of Domino 3 ahead of their dinner meeting with Ann and Ellie (who don't know). Are you with me?

It was a pleasant evening in London's Shard restaurant as The Politician, The Banker and 2 journalist sat down for dinner.

Ann welcomed everyone although she had already been sitting down with Ellie before the journalists arrived.

"It's been somewhat of a hectic time hasn't it" Ann followed with.

Sarah and Simon looked at each other and both raised their eyes at the same time.

"Tomorrow it's going to get even more hectic" was Simon's opening words. With a brief pause he then added "we've been contacted by Domino 3".

It was the Minister and Banker to share looks this time but I think the best way of expressing that look is "FFS".

Ann questioned "not another letter just addressed to the Press surely?"

"No" said Sarah, "better in a way, a phone call and only made to our Editor Brad".

"A phone call!" both the other two ladies said in a higher than normal surprised tone. "How do you know it's not a hoax?"

"Would you like to hear it?" said Simon.

"What? you had time to record it and the caller didn't mind" asked Ellie.

"No quite the opposite, she suggested we did. Quite a sweet sounding Irish lady actually". Simon suddenly regretting his choice of words over such a serious matter.

"Well let's hear the next stage of chaos then please can we before we get into the really serious business before the probably even more serious business after this call is heard!"

With that, Sarah took the copy of the tape out and put it in her dictaphone and pressed play. They were in a private room in view of the sensitive nature of their intended discussion, another layer of sound proofing would not go amiss for this extra orderve though.

So our sweet Felicity was now being listened to by a member of the cabinet who's daily work place was the Houses of Parliament.

I think I've run out of descriptions for shocks on faces so let's just say the two ladies looked really really shocked.

When in such stage of shock, social media memes would be to 'have a glass of wine'. Yep that's what happened, both ladies taking one unusually large swig.

Ann said "ok your team have obviously had time to talk

about this already so give myself and Ellie the run down before we get into our expected chat".

Simon responded, "yes our editorial team meet regularly. We are going to print an entire transcript of the phone call. We can't take a chance it's not real but nothing has happened and November the 5th is a long way off. Our approach is that we will say it may be a hoax".

"The other thing is that we don't know if this Irish lady is really clever or a little silly. She asked for the entire transcript to be published but that also means everyone knows she has agreed to speak to our journalist Bill – that will include the police".

"Equally we don't know why she asked for Bill but our assumptions are that she liked his Domino 2 headline and story the best".

Ann questioned, "have you given this to Boris and the Police before you publish?"

"Yes" the two newspaper people said, "that is either happening now or has just happened".

"Brad will let the PM know that we are telling you both in this meeting" Simon responded.

"So tomorrow then, we all wake up, if in fact any of us get any damn sleep, we wake up to a National soap opera of debates!" Ann exclaimed *(I couldn't have phrased that better myself Ann)*.

Sarah added, "yes our team think that of all the 3

Dominos this particular one is going to hit home in the heart of millions and cause rumbles afar" *(now Sarah, you are not wrong but I don't think that any length of wine break for my readers is going to help them fathom exactly how far)*.

The other important point that Brad asked us to raise is that leaves the door open for Domino 4 and the whole Domino story is going to explode because this Irish lady *(even Sarah was going to add "sweet" but stopped herself mid flow)* has said they are all connected".

Have I used the phrase 'penny dropped yet '? If not, the penny dropped on one Politician and Banker – both wondering if Domino 4 could do their sectors any more damage.

During this enthralling discussion, before the intended enthralling discussion Ellie had finished her glass of wine (it was a large one). It's true that a glass of wine calms you down and helps you think. Ellie was about to prove that.

"Right" said Ellie in an authoritative CEO manner "I think the fact that we are meeting now is fortunate then. I believe that what Ann and I were going to share with you might help in all Domino cases, including this unexpected one".

Ellie looked at Ann in a sort of a mind sharing way and said "Ann, as you are the Politician I think you should summarise what Boris and the Cabinet have said and what the three Bank CEO's feel and then I'll chip in how I think this helps all".

"Ok" Ann said and also had composed herself (although secretly thinking of all the bloody nuisance disorganised unplanned development going on in her country hide away was causing).

"I think you journalists are going to be surprised and I think I can see where Ellie is going to go with this. The fact that you have been contacted solely by Domino 3 is an excuse as to why we have met with you first rather than wait for a Downing Street release.

So in short summary. Boris is announcing Parliament will meet but not only that, he will say the cabinet are in favour of such a law. And not only that the three CEO's are also agreeing that they think a suitable quantified law is correct.

"The look of utter surprise in the two newspaper people faces was good for another photo shoot. That surprise had not ended though.

"There is more though. The three CEOS have agreed to call and chair a meeting will all the banks to re-evaluate exactly how much was lost to shareholders in failed institutions where their customers were passed on to another banking institution. They can't agree anything at this stage but the intention is to work with me in seeing if we can come up with any type of subsequent offer to shareholders of the past.

I MUST emphasise, this is an exercise not a guarantee."

The journalists both said "that's brilliant" and Sarah continued "but how does that help with Domino 1?"

"Well" said Ann "there is even more the Cabinet had a chance to talk following comments from myself and Ellie.

Although we can't be seen to be given in to demands from wreck-less acts we all agreed to take a breath, sit and think of the wider picture on the dominos and their issues.

If we are good honest people we think they have valid points and many wrongs have been done and never corrected or tried to do so when it's too late. They are frustrated that they did not know how else to affect change so they've gone for public opinion via the social media and press.

Public opinion is how elections are won. These dominos are very clever people and not really asking a lot and if we did our jobs diligently in the first place then maybe we would not be here today.

So on Domino 1 the cabinet was easily able to talk about our donations to Africa and other countries and discuss 'where does the money go' – not too far away from Domino 2's little ploy. We even talked the same about Band Aid and how the crisis is still not resolved despite going on for years and years. The issue is not just money, the amount and where it's spent, it's the right people from many places in the right place and with an actual plan.

I'll pause there just to quickly let you think of how that's similar to Domino 3 whilst I fill up our wine glasses" she added.

"So anyway, Boris is going to announce that he wants to hold a meeting with the African Parliaments to discuss how and what they would need to stop trophy hunting and assistance in anti poaching. He will then say he would conduct a meeting of the UN to agree a structured plan to oversee what is needed including financial support.

You see, Simon and Sarah, if we senior people step back from how we do things now and realise that the particular 'how' doesn't change or solve things, in fact we hide things, then we don't really need the press to write a feature article. We already know what should be done and can be done. Our CEOs knew what could have been done in 2008 for example and I certainly know our Africa contributions could do with a plan and an end result.

It's a sad admittance from the worlds politicians, our billionaires and our entrepreneurs as a world group that we can't stop trophy hunting or end the famine in Africa."

If Bill Cartwright (journalist) was sitting here right now, he would have fallen off his chair as he was already mid flow in a totally different response to the dominos than requested. He would have wondered if Ellie and Ann had met the same guy he did on his journalistic travels one time.

"Blimey, that's got to be the quickest most sensible solution to anything I've heard in my lifetime. Our readers would love that even if such a release had come out without the dominos intervention". An excited voice from Simon explained.

All four looked at each other as . . . guess what readers . . . the pennnnnny dropppped!

"But" he said "how does that help Domino 3?"

Ellie interjected from Ann at this point confident they were going to be naturally on the same wave length. "Well your journalist Bill Cartwright, correct? Is going to meet with Domino 3. If you think about it she just wants to know the issue is being looked at and now and how. It's not hard to say that indeed the whole development issue is being looked at.

There is discussion already of this new Corporate Law and that will cover all sectors including property developers and I'm sure that Ann (as the new "Problem Minister) can agree to call an urgent overview of development plans and was intending to do so before Domino 3.

Ann was nodding and saying "exactly".

The Dominos want to see that good people are not doing nothing anymore.

All those they are possibly accusing are either senior people, billionaires and politicians and I think we are all big and brave enough to take that on the chin, challenge it or do something about it. Those choosing still to do nothing will have a rather nasty evil social media following.

Bill would have wished he was at that meeting as his article would have been finished in half the time.

The meeting ended with all 4 feeling that a sense of good had been achieved by the discussion alone.

Some good people were going to do something.

CHAPTER 20

Domino Sensation

So readers you would have already known the main out-come of the earlier Daily Digest Editorial meeting,

Julie Harper was indeed doing a little Irish jig under the table. Bill was at home researching for articles so he had heard the taped call over the conference phone.

Same issues as before we're discussed but Bill had asked how he would be contacted by Domino 3. Brad said "she never mentioned Bill but keep your phone on and take all calls even if unknown ones".

They agreed to stick to the same story headline of "for evil men and women to succeed it takes good men and women to do nothing".

But this would be a sub headline under 'Daily Digest contacted by Domino 3 – the modern Guy Fawkes'.

Well that morning when that was published there was a domino sensation. The original taped conversation was actually put on line. It may or may not have been a real

Irish voice but very few people challenged it. Anyone who knew Felicity would not have an inkling that was her.

In fact the social media memes and conversations and groups 'blew up'.

One of the Memes was a picture of a middle aged Irish lady (annotated by a four leaf clover in her hair) flying a crop duster plane over the Houses of Parliament and dropping a whole pile of horse manure on top. The caption read 'now is this where the shit dump is'.

The most Google searched fancy dress and guy fawkes costumes were those featuring dominos.

Another Meme appeared with "Domino Woman" super imposed over a picture of the Marvels Avengers with the caption "Move over Captain Marvel – Domino Woman is here".

Even the actual sale of dominos had increased and it was gathered that these were going to be for pranks or actual joke gifts.

You would not believe how many comments were "can't wait for Domino 4" and on this thread people had uploaded a Meme of Thunderbird 4 overwritten with Domino 4.

This particular Domino, this sweet Irish lady, had hit the heart of the U.K. for sure.

What Felicity Myers would have been relishing in was how much arse covering and panicking was going on across the country council offices. Local Councillors especially were looking back at all their claimed expenses and some indeed were worried about further investigation into their income status.

There were contractors on these huge sites now feeling guilty about the good work that they were doing but that memes showed them under the caption "helping build ruined lives and communities".

The contractors and skilled workmen were good people but they knew their millionaire bosses didn't give a hoots about infrastructure and services.

Seriously readers it is at this point I will forgive you if even in your own minds you cannot imagine how chaotic this was.

With the amount of social media traffic and the very first possible identity of a domino, who knew the others, the world was literally on baited breath or tender hooks or edge of their seat or the whole lot.

And of course the news did not take long to reach Sonia Parker and William and Benjamin Mud. This was lightening fast social media after all.

Even they had to smile at the third of their unknown trio and were quite pleased at what she said. They thought they would like that sweet little Irish woman. And indeed Felicity would like them.

They each wondered if in fact one day they might meet?

CHAPTER 21

Bill cartwright Domino 4?

B ill was crazy excited that he might have a meeting with a Domino. Julie was crazy excited about that Domino too and asked if there was anyway she could join and meet this modern day real super hero.

Following the news of Domino 3 Bill had reflected on the research he was doing for the two previous articles and a sudden realisation came into his journalist brain.

'Sudden realisation is a writers way of not using "the penny dropped".

He had turned up to another meeting early that next morning quite excited about his plan.

Brad had offered Bill to commence the meeting with his views.

Bill stood up for this and commenced "It has dawned on me (aka penny has dropped) that the Dominos don't need us to write a feature article really. Yes it would be great but we don't need to. They have got the attention they wanted already. What they would prefer is some action on their issues, that's probably why they have said 60 days".

"I bet Domino 3, if she makes contact with me, is going to say just that. That sweet lady isn't going to destroy the Houses of Parliament and we all know that. Her need was to get he phone call published. We all know from the media chaos out there that such publication worked".

Brad interrupted "it's worked for us too, another best day sales".

Bill continued "They have gone from being a murderer and thief to super hero's on many on line chats and even before Domino 3 it was the minority of social media against them.

So they are looking for publication of proactive action and I don't mean just to their issues.

They are seeing who still does nothing without them or more dominos pushing further'

There is no point in papers competing for a prize to meet Dominos 1 and 2. That again was just really clever.

So, I want to draft a front page article addressed to the Dominos and see if I can get them to respond in agreement and then also to stop if our published action is sufficient.

So what do you guys think?"

Bill had not yet heard about the meeting his good

friends and colleagues Simon and Sarah had with the Politician and Banker.

Brad had already been told and he Simon and Sarah looked at each other with friendly disbelief smiles. The editor said "Simon and Sarah, I think one of you should fill Bill and the rest of the team in on your dinner meeting last night".

And so they repeated what they had been told nearly to a round of applause at the end. Such incredible high level action on three really serious subjects by the most senior people possible.

Well, both Bill and Julie, were ecstatic.

Bill said out really loud, holding the edition of his first article "for evil men and woman to succeed it takes good men and women to do nothing".

All in unison around the table said "exactly!! – *lots of sounds of pennies dropping at this point.*

Bill then went onto say something that astounded his audience. He said "yes I want to write the communication to the Dominos from us but I don't want to mention the actual action agreed/stated by the PM, Ann and Ellie.

I want to say that action is being taken and then in the next few days, as soon as is possible, hold a meeting with the Editors of all Newspapers and the National Union of journalists.

It is only fair all have the right to write good news stories as the dominos want at the same time.

Unity in the press is likely to achieve more than outright competition. After all, we all write about the same stories at the same time every day anyway. It's just that stories come to us, we are never proactive enough to co-ordinate stories that help the public on local or major worldwide issues.

If journalists met and said 'let's write a story to end Trophy hunting' we all probably could and they would all be different and hence all readable and we would know whom to pressure to get things done, we have contacts in every country".

Brad and the team agreed. It seemed to them that despite the immense near hysteria caused in so many corners of so many sectors and across every household that although these stories will be remembered for years there might actually be a positive end very soon.

Bill had no idea at this stage as he left the conference room that he might be Domino 4 and his role was not yet finished. He had a strange urge though to end his article 'signed Domino 4'. Maybe he would?

CHAPTER 22

Dancing feet

As Bill left the office and hit the welcome fresh air of the outside (London could not be truly classified as fresh air) he felt relieved and excited.

He had not thought of his exact message to the Dominos yet and in fact had too many ideas and he needed to drop some and focus.

'Now you and I readers would, when head is full, take a tea or wine break but for Bill it was a nice cold pint'

Not too far ahead was a pub called 'The Penny Drop' and Bill was a regular. As he went to push the pub door open a delightful lady said "I think you and I are due to meet Mr Cartwright" it was said in a very typical middle class English accent.

"I'm sorry? – I'm not sure who you are" – responded Bill.

"Well top of the morning, do me a jig and fly me crop duster over the top of a rainbow if you wouldn't mind" she replied in a very convincing Irish accent.

Bill could not help but smile "Domino 3 he whispered?"

With that Felicity handed him a Domino with one blank square and the other with 3 white dots. She laughed an Irish laugh and said "to be sure twas me, one of those tousands of idiots who went and bought a set of dominos this morning".

They both laughed and Bill widened the door open for Domino 3 to enter first and then went to the bar.

Bill asked what she would like to drink and she replied "I've been taking a lot of wine breaks lately but nows not the time to stop that habit so I'll have a large Pinot please".

Bill could not help recall how many times this lady had been referred to as sweet. Here she was in the flesh, as sweet as ever.

This lady, in Bills' eyes, was the epitome of a decent human being. A salt of the Earth, well but very casually dressed, calendar girl country type. He was not sure how such a brief meeting would draw him to that conclusion.

As they were sitting down, one beer, one wine, Bill said "it really is nice to meet you, why did you ask to speak to me?"

Her next words were to shock Bill – yes shock him far more than any of the previous days absolutely knock him down shocking dead days.

She said "Well Bill, you are Domino 4 aren't you" and with that secretly slid under a palm another Domino – one square blank and one with four white dots.

Bill looked at the Domino and he was silenced, truly silenced like in a trance. When he came to he had the real urge to say "yes" but he did not know why.

Felicity knew that look as she was never truly sure what made her say she was Domino 3.

After a few minutes and at least half a pint of his just pulled pint had gone Bill said "no – why do you say that "

She simply replied "I just think you are and I think you met someone I've met on travels who might be another domino".

The now truly flabbergasted journalist had a sneaky feeling he probably did.

"So" she said "here I am as promised, I said I would meet you so you knew who Domino 3 is, the rest is up to you now".

The first thing Bill had to ask was "do you really know who Domino 1 and 2 are?"

"No, not a clue but I wish I did"

Bill laughed. "And you are not going to destroy the Houses of Parliament are you?"

"No but I wish I was"

And they both laughed a hearty laugh.

These two were really a good man and woman

Bill looked honestly at Domino 3 and said "do you know what, I have no idea what else to ask at this time and I should, I'm a journalist".

Felicity said "I think that's because you already know the answers to anything you would ask any of the domino's Bill, that is why you are a journalist".

At that point an idea came to him but he had to get permission, he asked "Do you have much time and would you mind if a colleague of mine whom I trust entirely, and think you will like, could join us?"

"Bill my time is yours, no one else knows I've contacted you, no one suspected me to just turn up and I doubt you will call the police as that would end this interview. I think you will understand fully the importance of keeping promises and obligations. Feel free to include that point in any article you might like to write" and she winked a wink that only a mature intelligent, salt of the earth sweet lady could wink.

On that Bill called his colleague "hello are you still in the office?"

"Yes I am" came the reply.

Ok I'm in the pub down the road 'the Penny Drop' I'm in mid flow on my article but I need your help, can you come down but please make sure you are on your own as I have something confidential to talk to you about".

With intrigue the response came "I'm on my way, be there in ten".

When Julie Harper arrived she approached Bill at his table enthusiastically and looked at the lady with him quite curiously.

Bill greeted her with a smile, as did the pretty lady, and said "please sit down Julie and meet Domino 3".

Julie fell down but managed at the same time to put out an arm and hand and say "excited to see you".

Felicity shook her hand and said "nice to see such a young pretty, energetic face".

Julie thought 'how sweet'.

Bill ordered Julie a drink and said "Julie, as our youngest apprentice I thought you might like to have the task of interviewing our most famous story".

"Really! Oh my god".

The continued sweet look of Felicity gave Julie a welcoming and warm confidence.

"Ok what is your real name?" She commenced with.

Bill chastised himself 'bloody hell I haven't even thought to ask her real name!'

Felicity noticed the embarrassed look on his face. She replied "hello Julie my name is Felicity but as you can appreciate that is not to be published".

"Felicity, why do you think all the dominos are doing what they are doing?"

"To get the right people in the right positions to do something by the power of the decent press" came the reply

"Do you think you are succeeding?"

"Do you think we are succeeding will be a better answer than mine"

God this lady is quick and smart thought the two inter-viewers at the same time.

"Do you know if there will be anymore dominos?"

Bloody great question Bill thought.

Felicity looked at Bill, gave a sly Irish wink and said "i don't know to be honest, so again do you think there should be?"

Smarter than smart her drinking colleagues thought.

"Do you really know the other Dominos?"

"No I only know about Domino 4 but I don't think the press will hear from them".

"Why is that do you think?"

"Because I think Bill here will write an article that makes no need for it"

"And why do you think that?"

"Because he secretly thinks I'm a sweet lady as I think you do my sweet child".

All three laughed a hearty friendly laugh.

"So do you think the series of Dominos will end?"

"That is the best question ever, who knows?, there is someone I met a while ago who might be able to give you that answer".

"Who is that?"

"I can't remember his name so have to refer to him as the traveller but I do think the other dominos know him".

"What is your main wish from all of this?"

"That is easy, same as the others and I repeat . . . for the right people in the right place with the right power and or money to do the right thing.

For evil men and women to succeed it takes good men and women to do nothing".

"You are a good woman aren't you Felicity"

"Is that a question or a statement"

"A statement" said Julie.

All three smiled and took a swig of their drink, clinked glasses as if they had been friends all their lives.

Eventually Felicity said she had to leave now and wished them both luck with their article. She reminded them that the meeting was in confidence and her name was not to be given. So far all she had done was make a hoax call to a news desk and followed it up with a hoax meeting.

She was not the sweet lady who had just caused the biggest National Debate since Brexit.

Bill and Julie stood up and said "thank you".

Felicity exited with "what you do from here will decide wether, not just this country, but the world, will want to thank you or not".

Now, "top of the mornings to yuse both" reverting back to her Irish twin.

Julie hugged Bill after Felicity had left and said "thank you so much Bill, I really appreciate that".

He responded "you did me a favour, at that time you was the right person to be in the right place at the right time and not me".

Julie thought he was hinting to the fact that maybe Felicity viewed upon her as her daughter asking the questions.

Bill said "right we both deserve another drink and then I need to get back and write this article, would you mind not telling anyone that you were here and that I invited you here".

"Not a problem Bill 'mums the word"

That night the three new friends were going to sleep more soundly than normal, all because they felt some good was being done by good people.

CHAPTER 23

Hello Dominos

The following day Bill had shown to the Editorial Team his message to the Dominos he wanted published. He also declared that he had been contacted by Domino 3, out the blue, as he left the office last night.

> *'I don't really need to fill you readers in the Q and A of that as you know the answers to the same questions. I will just add though that only Bill and Julie will be able to refer to Domino 3 as Felicity.'*

Upon agreement, he had contacted the Chairman of the National Union of Journalist and explained he was releasing an exclusive. That he wanted as many members of the NUJ to attend a group meeting within the next four days if possible.

This is what his simple 'article' said:-

Hello Dominos,

I hope you are in a place where this message finds you.

The world, the press and politicians have heard you far and wide.

We here don't think you are actually needing your feature articles published that you have asked for. We think you are seeing if actual action can be taken rather than writing about the past and what should have happened.

I myself have personally met with Domino 3, as they promised they would and that meeting is confidential and the authorities have been told the threat was a hoax but not the importance of their issues. As there is no longer any threat from Domino 3 the authorities have said the meeting can remain confidential.

What I can tell you is that actual action is going to be taken far better than any article a journalist can write.

That action should not be reported by one journalist like myself though, the world of journalists need to be involved so we have arranged a meeting for just that.

So, if you and the worlds public stay tuned you will see that some very good men and women have decided not to do nothing. Not because of any threat but because the penny dropped that perhaps for too long good men and women in the right place at the right time with the right money or power have done nothing, or simply not the right thing or not enough.

If you could, in some way, signal you have read this and do agree with our assumptions then please do so. A release in all papers will soon be following once the worlds journalist have met.

Thank you

Signing off Domino 4

The message was published front page and for consecutive days in a row The Digest had more sales than their previous high before the run of Domino coverage.

CHAPTER 24

Quiet for a while

After the article was published all went quiet for a few days or so but not in terms of social media chatter. There was no sign yet when the Domino stories would let up.

Banks had opened new accounts for every zeroed account so all was considered ok.

Trophy Hunting was still banned in Kruga and behind the scenes U.K. government was leading other countries on the Africa issues and funding project lead by the very capable Ann Drake.

Ann (now 'problem minister') had called for a full review from the Secretary of State and every head of council and planning departments. She insisted that they all gave statistics and proof that every town expanded by development had sufficient infrastructure. If not, why not and also where has all the money gone?

The public wasn't too sure about Bill's sign off as Domino 4 and some were waiting for the real domino 4 to show. Others were waiting for Domino 5!!

The Memes on Domino 5 were already in full flow and also another Meme from Thunderbirds. Thunderbird 5 was the out in space Thunderbird and thousands, if not millions, thought Domino 5 would take task at Elon Musk. Having billions to spend on sending humans to destroy Mars rather than spend their billions on solving many of Earths current problems, not just its destruction by humans.

Anyhow, life seemed to be settling back down.

The Butcher-Jones husband and wife team had not solved the little weed issue yet but the pressure was off for a short while.

They were meeting in their regular cafe one lunchtime to discuss new possibilities to the solution when a pair of familiar faces came and sat opposite them.

William and Benjamin Mud greeted them with a smile and said "long time no see you in here".

"Yes indeed" came the joint response.

Shannon added "wow, so lovely to see you both, what have you been up to, anything exciting?"

The twins smiled and said "this and that, still redundant developers".

"Oh sorry guys we are not taking contract work anymore because of the extra security risk following this Domino and Banking issue which I'm sure you are aware of".

"No worries" they both replied. William said, we are not

actually looking for work. In fact we knew you might be in here still regularly so we were looking for you".

"Oh really, that's nice, what's the reason? Do you want to employ us?" laughed Shannon.

"That would be great, another day maybe, but no we want to do you a favour but you must swear not to say anything of our meeting".

Husband and wife looked at each other in not just surprise but also as an immediate 'do you think we can do so' type of question look.

They both said "sure, what's the favour?"

With that the Twins stood up, handed the duo an envelope and said "we have always liked you both and for evil men and women to succeed it takes good men and women to do nothing" and then left as quickly as they entered.

Shannon opened the envelope and inside were two dominos. One had a blank square and another with two white dots. The other had a blank square and four white dots and attached to it was a small memory card with the word "solution" written on it.

The Husband and wife team smiled at each other, patted each other on the knee and both reflected on what a hard and horrible time those two good men had at the industry they did so much good work for.

They would make a call to Bill Cartwright and also explain to Adam Rudd that they received an untraceable email from Domino 2 simply with the word "Solution" in it and the message – pass to Domino 4.

. . . .

A few days after in Africa a dear friend of Sonia Parker, called Sharma, was on one of her poacher patrols.

Suddenly a silent shot whistled someway above her head and hit the tree behind her.

She thought she had had a lucky escape and laid low, eagle eyes out on the distance, all she could see a long long way out were trees moving which was just monkeys or birds she thought. After a few minutes she also thought what a terrible shot.

When she looked up at the tree behind she saw the bullet had hit dead centre of a small carved target. Underneath that target was also a carved domino with one square black and one square with one painted dot. Underneath in really small exceptionally carved words was:-

*"For evil men and women to succeed it takes
good men and women to do nothing"*

underneath that there were 4 painted white dots.

Sharma knew all the news from the U.K. and the dominos story. She knew what the message was and who it was for. She also thought 'what a bloody great shot!

An old friend of hers could shoot that good, not seen her for years after her husband and daughter sadly died. So so sad. Be nice to catch up with her again and see how she is doing, such a good woman.

....

In her country recluse Felicity Myer was looking for a new home further away.

And that weekend she was looking forward to seeing a new friend she had met. A young eager journalist who had agreed to take up a National story on her towns issues as an example of the wider impact across all the country

CHAPTER 25

Time for Change

Bill Cartwright stood in front of at least 2,000 editors and journalists in the massive Barbican conference centre London.

A few days before he had made another front page article about being sent a message by Domino 1 and 2. In his coverage he had indicated that as far as he was aware the Dominos were individuals who had never met.

The social media chatter continued at fever pitch, many were sad that still no one knew who any of the dominos were. Domino 5 stories were still in full flow.

Debates on Trophy Hunting, Corporate Greed and Corruption, and of course Housing Planning were main topics across more than breakfast tables.

Where the penny had fully dropped in some very large corporations the CEO's had created a new board position of 'Ethical Director' Their task to purposefully challenge anything they thought could be considered greed, corrupt or just unethical. Those who did so had the best customer and shareholder feedback for years. It was also prudent with the new Corporate Corruption (Domino) law pending.

The great Barbican Hall was alive with chatter and the room full of journalistic expectations. There were representatives from at least 60 countries amongst the biggest writer gathering since the NUJ began.

Bill stood up and commenced.

"My friends, Ladies, Gentlemen and esteemed colleagues.

Thank you for attending today.

I am sure that like I and our editorial teams you have had a busy few weeks and many many meetings.

As journalists it's always hectic but equally I think we were probably all actually excited.

I asked for this meeting as by fortune it seemed I and my colleagues were party or privy to new information before other papers or totally new just to us, including the Domino 3 meeting.

Our editorial team had decided that the main aim of the Dominos was not to really put us on trial but to a test.

Domino 3 admitted to me that their objective had already been met by the publication of their requests. They knew that if it touched the public's hearts and mind in the same way as theirs that Social Media would do just a good a job as a feature article.

Of course we all now know that Domino 1 and 2 also agreed by now.

These were 3 separate people who somehow, by luck, fortune or intellect managed to unite with each other. *(A traveller knew otherwise).*

Media, politicians and even bankers were put to the ultimate test.

That test was 'will you still do nothing'?

Well today you would have been handed the official release from Ann Drake with headline news stories of:

1. Corporate Corruption Law (aka Domino Law)
2. Africa world task force
3. New Minister as a focal point for citizen problems caused by wrongs not being corrected or identified.

And on that point my friends I would urge you to reflect on that as journalists. What would Dominos 5, 6, 7 8 and 9 and more have to investigate? We should know. We should unite.

We have to remember it's our readers who we represent and stories should no longer be biased because of a political preference or tit for tat nor because of fear of upsetting advertisers or corporations.

What's been proven is that stories that inspire and

relate to readers increase substantially our sales and subscriptions.

There is so much wrong with this world and it's been proven that we can be part of the cure.

The floor will now be open for any questions or to simply raise topics that are worth investigating and where two or more journalists from differing papers are needed then so be it.

It's time for a change and to act now, to be ahead of Dominos.

It's time that 'good men and women no longer do nothing'.

Thank you.

With that every attendee not standing stood and applauded and each and every attendee had an appetite. Sooooo much to write about and investigate.

CHAPTER 26

The End?

After an exhilarating and rewarding conference Bill was absolutely shattered mentally and physically. It had been one of the most hectic periods of his career.

He was pleased to have found his way back to The Penny Drop and pleased that Julie Harper had agreed to join him again.

They reflected fondly of all the recent events and in particular their meeting with Felicity.

Julie said to Bill "I guess this is where the media industry say we enter a lull period after the storm?"

He smiled but before he could reply, his phone rang and he thought he had better answer it.

"Hello Bill, you might not remember me but we met on our travels one time"

Bill did remember and knew there was to be no lull just yet.

About the Author

I hope you enjoyed this first novel by Ann R Quay which is an Alias of the real me, Colin Baker, for particular novels of certain subjects including:-

And so it begins.

Did your story and characters follow the same as mine?

I don't fill my writing with too much descriptive padding such as of people, places and events and that is why you will find my novels shorter than others.

I prefer the readers to create their own atmosphere and people with just a guide from me.

Hopefully then you don't speed read and skip bits as if so you might miss important clues.

Did you guess the real connection between the Traveller and not just the dominos but the other main characters in this novel?

If you think you know then send your thoughts via email to **annrquayauthor@gmail.com**

The winner will have a one to one chat with me (the real Ann Quay) and a signed copy of the book.

Judges decision is final and you have to be quick, entries close on 5th November 2023

And remember readers:-

For evil men and woman to succeed it takes
good men and women to do nothing.

Lightning Source UK Ltd.
Milton Keynes UK
UKHW012206270722
406469UK00002B/58